Tales From the Lost Coast

Cecelia Holland, Ed.

Copyright © 2011 Rain All Day Writers

All rights reserved.

ISBN: 1461082226
ISBN-13:9781461082224

Tales From the Lost Coast

Short stories by the Rain All Day Writers,
edited and with a preface by Cecelia Holland
with illustrations by Heather Emke

FIRST EDITION

CONTENTS

	Preface	i
1	Kid's Game, by Cecelia Holland	3
2	Sorrow Eater, by Aline Faben	7
3	Trim Job, by Monica Hubbard	16
4	The One you Don't See, by Rick Markgraf	24
5	North Coast Vapor, by Shari Snowden	30
6	Azaria, by June Nessler	31
7	She's Alive! by Shari Snowden	37
8	Adventures in Birdwatching, by Anthony Westkamper	49
9	A Friend in Deed, by Rick Markgraf	54
10	Based on Actual Events, by Lisa Baney	58
11	Talia, by June Nessler	63
12	Enter Y for "Yes," by Anthony Westkamper	71
13	A Swig of Coffee, by Shari Snowden	76
14	A Year to Forget, by June Nessler	78
15	A Wide Spot in the Road, by Anthony Westkamper	85
16	Deep Down Things, by Lisa Baney	92
17	Miscast, by Rick Markgraf	105

PREFACE

The Rain All Day Writers

Our group began a few years ago, in Monica Hubbard's store, Rain All Day Books, when it was still down an alley behind Main Street in Fortuna. Some people left, new people joined, but there have always been about six of us, meeting every two weeks to share our work, listen to each other's work, and talk about reading and books.

Out of those meetings *Tales From the Lost Coast* has come. Each of the stories is set somewhere on the North Coast, and the voices in them are definitely Humboldt voices, from the motorcyclist out on Highway 36 in Tony Westkamper's "Wide Spot in the Road" to the townspeople in Aline Faben's "Sorrow Eater." Both these stories refer to the past, to an older wisdom, part of the general spookiness of Humboldt County; but then, many of these stories are pretty spooky.

Often in the most commonplace terms. Lisa Baney's "Based on Actual Events" has a scene in Winco; Rick Markgraf's "Miscast" is set both in a stifling community theater dressing room and at Centerville Beach. Shari Snowden's lovely little "A Swig of Coffee" happens in Los Bagels in Old Town.

The redwoods are everywhere, home of ghosts and witnesses to truth, as in Snowden's "She's Alive!" and her poem "North Coast Vapor." You'll find yourself in the deceptive quiet of a small town Sunday in my own "Kid's Game," and swimming in the treacherous and magnificent coast in Markgraf's "The One You Don't See," and watching the wildlife—sort of—at Hookton Slough in Westkamper's "Adventures in Birdwatching." June Nessler takes us all camping in the Trinity Alps in "Azaria," and in Monica Hubbard's "Trim Job" the heroine also goes into the woods, but for a rather different reason.

What strikes me about these stories is their humanity. The people in these stories reach out to each other even across some pretty remarkable boundaries. The dialogue in Tony Westkamper's "Enter Y for Yes" is all the more intense for being in code. Several of the stories involve communicating with people who aren't really there—and in many cases, the ghosts answer back.

We live in small towns. The glimpses of other people are spare, but often searingly strong. The everyday-ness, the honesty of small towns shines through all these stories. Even when these stories take flights of fancy there is a human scale. Over all, these stories seem grounded in a sense of the ultimate goodness of ordinary life, a sustaining faith that we can talk to each other, that we have something vital in common, on which we can build and which will nurture us.

The Rain All Day Writers is such a community.

Maybe the group is so important to us because we came looking for it. We all moved here from somewhere else—some have been here thirty years or more, but we aren't "from here." We chose this place. In Humboldt County, where the trees outnumber the people, we've found manageable lives, out of reach of the hectic pretensions of the city. Here the relationship between nature and human seems about right, the human modest, and the natural world enormous around us, sometimes cradling and nurturing us, and sometimes (in windstorms and floods and power outages) throwing us back to the Stone Age. Here, in contact with the sky, the forests and the river, the broad vistas of hillsides and river valley, we know who we are, and we bloom. These stories are from that garden of minds.

Cecelia Holland
Fortuna, California
April, 2011

KID'S GAME

by Cecelia Holland

When I pulled into the driveway my husband was standing there waiting, and I could tell just from the look of him something was wrong.

I got out of the car and he said, "Where's Jenny?"

"Jenny," I said, with a familiar twitch of alarm. "She spent the night at Alice's house."

"Yeah," he said. "Alice's dad called up here looking for her. Alice told him they were staying with us. The last he saw of them was letting them off in front of the movie theater last night."

"Unh," I said. I lifted the groceries out of the car, a bag in each arm.

"If you'd keep her under control--"

"Here. Take these inside. I'm going to look for her." I pushed the bags into his arms and got back into the car.

I drove down to the movie theater on Main Street, as if I were a dog who could pick up the scent. It was Sunday and Fortuna was empty, especially around the movie theater. I turned down past the park. In front of the little depot museum two boys on skateboards were bouncing on and off the curb. I knew one from Jenny's class, and I swerved over and called to him.

He drifted toward me on his board, stepped off, and with a deft kick of his heel sat it on end. He had a huge scab on his left arm above the elbow. I asked him if he'd seen Jenny.

"Not today." He had the edgy look of a kid afraid of incriminating himself.

"When, then?"

"Last night."

"At the movies?"

He shrugged, looking not at me. Ten feet away the other boy watched us steadily.

"Who was she with?"

"Alice Grimshaw. And Myrna Bly."

"Unh," I said. I knew Myrna Bly by sight, and Jenny had talked about her; she had an alarming reputation for a fourteen-year-old. "But you haven't seen them since."

"Un-uh." He was edging away. The skateboard dropped flat and he stepped on it and was immediately in motion. His friend followed him. I went off and toured the park and drove around a while, finding nothing, and went home.

Beth was in the kitchen, making herself breakfast, the only seventeen year old in the world still wearing footie pajamas. The bags of groceries were on the counter, and I began putting the food away. Beth looked at me, a fork in her hand, and said, "What's wrong?"

"Jenny's taken off again. There's orange juice now."

"Do you need help?"

"Do you know Myrna Bly?"

"Mom." She gave me a firm, rebuking look and turned back to scrambling eggs. "Jenny will come home, Mom. Go and watch football with Dad."

I went into the den, where Jack reclined in front of a stack of six TV's, each on a different football game. I sat down in the other chair.

"Have you heard anything?" I asked.

"You shouldn't let her hang out with that kid," Jack said. "I've told you that a hundred times. How often has she done this?"

I tried watching the little men running around on the screens but my stomach felt bad. I couldn't sit still. I went out to my car and drove downtown again. As long as I was looking, she wasn't lost.

The Sunday quiet lay on the town like a spell. I wandered through the warren of beat-up houses around the mill and turned down 12th Street. Surely I would feel her presence. If I just drove by the right house I would know she was there. On L Street by the old laundromat I saw another kid from Jenny's class, a rail of a girl in a camisole and lots of eye makeup.

She hadn't seen Jenny. She hadn't seen Alice. When I mentioned Myrna Bly she looked away down the street.

"She's friends with Francie."

"Francie," I said.

"She lives up there." She pointed toward the corner. "Cross from the bank."

Across the parking lot from the Bank of America was a gaunt old clapboard building with a false front. I had not realized that people lived there. I went around the building and found steps; I swallowed hard, getting up the nerve to climb them. At the top I went into a dark hallway, the walls and battered doors on either side scrawled with graffiti.

The third door I knocked on opened, and I said into the crack, "I'm looking for my daughter, Jenny Bolt. Somebody told me--"

The man beyond the sliver of open doorway turned and called, "Francie!"

He opened the door wider, a man my age in frayed jeans. The girl who came up beside him was scrawny and Jenny's age and masked in makeup. I said, "I'm looking for Jenny Bolt."

She shrugged. Behind her, the man, her father maybe, said, "Francie, help the lady, her girl's lost."

Her eyes shone at me through the crust of makeup. Open sesame. I said, "What about Alice Grimshaw? Myrna Bly?"

"Myrna," she said, suddenly spontaneous. "I hate her. She took my boyfriend."

I jumped on this one positive. "Where is she now?"

"I'll bet she's with my boyfriend!"

"Francie," her father said.

"I'll show you," Francie said to me. "But we have to drive."

I looked at her father, who was nodding. He said, "You have a car?" I realized he'd been this way before, and we were on the same side.

"Yes," I said. "I'll bring her straight home."

In the car, I expected Francie to steer me to some other part of Fortuna, but she said, "We have to go to Ferndale."

"Ferndale!" I turned onto Main Street and drove to the freeway. "Where did you meet this boyfriend?"

"Around," she said. From the side, her eyelashes looked like tarantulas.

We crossed the bridge and drove over the farmlands, and halfway to Ferndale she said, "Turn here." That road led through more flat grassy meadows, past a hayrack, an old collapsing barn. A scent of mown alfalfa swept in through the window. The ditch was full of wild radish, purple and white.

"Turn here," she said, and I drove into a dirt lane. Ahead, across a muddy lot filled with a huge stack of tires, was another barn.

"Stop," she said. "I'll go."

I stopped, and she darted out of the car.

I began wondering how long I should wait before I went in there myself; I wondered what I could try next. Then Francie was running back into sight, with three other girls, down past the stack of tires toward the lane. I started the car and drove up to meet them and Jenny rushed toward me, Alice, Myrna and Francie behind her, all giggling.

I wanted to hug her and beat her up both at once. Instead I packed them into the car and over the river to Fortuna and took each one home. When Jenny and I were finally alone I said, "What exactly do you think you were doing?"

She shrugged. "It was Myrna's idea. I'm glad you came, Mom. He was chasing us around with his hand down his pants and I didn't know how to get home."

"Why do you do this? This is crazy. You could have been hurt." Worse. Thinking of what might have happened I felt sick to my stomach. All these kids seemed to be moving on some different plane from mine, wilder and simpler. I clutched the wheel. "How did you get over there?"

Jenny lifted one shoulder, her face clear as sunshine. "Some guy took us, after the movie. They were nice. They milk cows. We slept on the floor. Nobody bothered us until this morning."

I turned into our driveway, seeing Jack waiting on the back porch. Obviously Alice's father had called him with the news, and he came yelling down the driveway. Jack adhered to the bellow and threaten school of parenting.

"Get to your room, girl. I'll talk to you later!"

She stalked past him. "Leave me alone!"

To me, he said, "This is your fault."

Over his shoulder, I saw Jenny smile at me, wide and pleased. It came to me she had enjoyed this, that she loved the excitement. She knew how to get out of her room. Nothing we did would stop her. In that sunny smile I saw the long and scary road ahead. Jack was still screaming at me and I went past him toward the house.

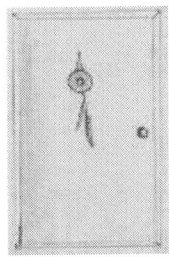

SORROW EATER

by Aline Faben

The dark narrow road wound between the redwoods. She sensed that something was on the road ahead. Her headlights picked out a laughing white face and a bicycle crashed into her tiny convertible, a body lay twisted, a bike wheel turned slowly in the headlight's glare.

The highway patrolman told her the name of the drunken cyclist who had changed her life by ending his own. For days she tried to complete the writing project that was due in weeks, but a face haunted her.

On the fourth morning, Roberta spoke sternly to her mirrored self. She was pale and her mid-brown hair stuck out in greasy clumps. Time to get out of the house.

"You're a reporter!" she told herself. "Investigate!"

She bathed and pulled on the least dirty jeans from the pile on the floor.

She went first to the village diner. Dottie, the proprietor and cook, kept working, chopping vegetables for a salad. Rangy and practical, she wore jeans and a tee-shirt and a ball-cap over her short gray hair.

"That's a tricky road," she said. "Luke knew as well as anyone – lived here most of his life."

"Then why was he dressed in black while riding his bike?" Roberta complained, shrugging off her sweater and shifting on her stool.

"He drank," Dottie said, chopping onions, barely weeping. "He got stupid."

The bitter coffee made Roberta wince. "The highway cop said it could be a form of suicide."

"That's not enough for you?"

"It keeps happening, in my head. I can't sleep." Roberta clawed her damp hair back from her face.

"What do you want from me?" Dottie suspended her knife above the white cutting board and faced her.

"Who was this guy? Seems like you all knew him. I didn't."

"You did."

"What?"

"You met him, anyway. You talked to him. I served the both of you coffee – a while back. Soon after you got here, I guess."

"I don't remember!"

"You had just come—likely he was part of the blur."

"What happened? Help me find a memory," Roberta begged.

"It was typical Luke. He was cute, and girls liked him."

"Do you have a photo?"

Dottie waved her knife toward the side wall of the diner. "Check the wall of fame." A checkerboard of photos nearly covered the unpainted drywall.

"He flirted with you," Dottie continued. "You seemed interested for a while, but I knew what would happen then."

"What do you mean?"

"He was like that. He would be OK -- talk like anyone -- charming, when he tried. He was cute, with pretty black hair and blue eyes -- and then, after a while, the crazy would come out. People got that squirmy feeling – that there was something wrong with him – and they'd edge away, have some place to go, like you. You jumped into your little car and skedaddled. So, when's it gonna be fixed?"

"I don't know. I've got that stupid loaner. Makes these twisty roads more treacherous than they would be in the Miata."

Dottie rolled her eyes. "Spoiled bitch."

Dented pickups were good enough around here.

"I'll never feel the same about it, after this. They have to send to Santa Rosa or Japan for a new windshield, bumper, and hood. I don't know if I'll keep it. You wouldn't think a bicyclist could mess up a car that bad."

It was wrong to mourn her car when a man's life had been lost. But still.

"It's such a tiny car, Hon. A wonder you weren't hurt, yourself."

"I have internal injuries."

Dottie put down her knife and poured Roberta another cup of coffee and one for herself. She sat down with her at the counter.

"Luke didn't belong anywhere. I'll miss him.... " She stopped, stared through the kitchen at the sun-washed yard beyond. "He didn't have an easy time. Sometimes he didn't have any place to live. He would stay with friends when they would have him. But they would get sick of him and throw him out."

Roberta went over to the wall and scanned the photos on it–snapshots of all sizes and shapes--until she found it--a group of guys gripping each other's shoulders to squeeze into the frame. She pried the tacks out of the drywall with the tip of her pocketknife.

Dottie pointed to a man on the edge of the blurry picture. A hank of dark hair hung over his eyes; he looked away from the camera.

"That's him," Dottie said. "It's not a good picture; you can't see how good looking he is."

Now Roberta remembered meeting him, talking with him at the window table while gazing out at the empty road. She had thought him good looking, but odd.

"Just lonely," she said, struck by the lost expression on the young man's face.

"Yeah," Dottie said, "You can see in the picture that he was lonely, but when times were noisy, you didn't notice."

Roberta knew what it was to be lonely in a crowd, but she had not responded to his longing. When she tacked the photo back into the wall, she noticed another, a square Polaroid print, faded to the aquarium blue of memory: Dottie standing in front of the diner with a tall man, arms around each other, each holding the end of a bill, likely their diner's first dollar. They were in love, defiant and proud, and going to make this diner work.

"Dottie?" She brought the photo back to Dottie, still at the counter, staring into space. "Who is this?"

Dottie glanced at the snapshot, looked away. "Not today. First Dennis, now Luke.... I can't."

"I'm an idiot."

"Go look at the basket caps in the case, Berta. They don't belong to me–I'm keeping them for Mary. She might help."

At first, Roberta had thought they were precious woven bowls. Now she saw the rhythmic black and red geometric designs on the yellowish ground. They had been made by local Native American women and were filled with a meaning that eluded her. Maybe Mary, whoever she was, would tell her--and Dottie thought it would be something to do with Luke.

Dottie said, bringing Roberta back, "Sometimes Luke stayed in the shed back of Jake's place. He sometimes gave him something to eat in exchange for work."

Jake ran the Quick Stop down the road, selling canned goods, toilet paper, snacks, milk, beer—stuff like that, the closest thing to a grocery in miles. Roberta had barely met him, though occasionally she bought five dollars worth of gas or an ice cream bar at his store.

She headed down to Jake's. She wondered if she wanted to know--or just feel better.

While she drove, the memory of talking to Luke at the diner continued to gel. Dottie's description and the blurry snapshot reminded her of chatting with a slim young man with a drooping forelock, clear, pale skin, startling blue eyes, and straight black eyebrows. She recalled finding his words quirky and arresting—some comment about the newspaper she'd been reading, the wars in Iraq and Afghanistan--until the links between his comments became tenuous. Instinct made her edge away from the young man whose thoughts didn't connect. She recalled now how she had glanced at Dottie, shrugged, and got up hurriedly. Dottie had smiled, seeing through her, even then.

There were no customers at the gas station when she arrived.

Jake said, responding to her question, "Everyone knew Luke."

Jake was in his fifties, of middle height, with medium gray hair, weather-beaten. His plaid flannel shirt hung open over the heavy paunch pushing above the belt of the jeans; his work boots were oil-stained. He looked like any other Humboldt County working man.

Roberta wasn't sure how to talk to Jake. He kept sweeping the sidewalk in front of the store when she approached with her notebook. She walked back and forth with him as he swept from the cement apron in front of the door to the pavement by the gas pumps and back.

"You helped him out, I heard," Roberta said.

"Who told you that?" Jake grumped.

"Dottie. She said sometimes Luke stayed in your shed out back, and you fed him."

Jake shrugged. "When there was burgers left over, been kep' hot all day, and I'd have to throw them out, sometimes he'd get some. No big deal, see? Didn't do no harm. I made him work for it. Sweep out the shop kinda thing. Anyway, Dottie did, too. She'd cook breakfast for him, give him coffee."

Jake was put out at being caught openhanded and wanted her to know Dottie had done the same. She glanced at the next item on her list.

"What did folks like about Luke?"

"Luke was OK." He stopped for a moment. "So he drank," he said, suddenly defensive. "So do most of 'em. Some folks don't like no one who's not rich. But we got plenty of folks with no dough or way of getting any. Folks with money—some of them aren't so great, neither."

She duly noted Jake's resentment of the undeserving rich. He had nailed her, who distrusted poor folks, women with unwashed hair, men whose jeans were ragged and dirty, or loiterers. She liked that he defended Luke.

"I'm trying to learn about Luke, because," she said, trying unsuccessfully to keep her voice level, "I killed him."

Jake stopped sweeping briefly. "You didn't mean to. Your bad luck you was there when he coasted down the road."

She'd have to get used to the fact that they knew every detail. Luke and the accident belonged to everyone in the village.

"I seen him do that in broad day, and it scared the bejesus outa me," Jake said.

"What did you do?"

"Honked at him. He laughed and give me the finger like usual."

"He was on the wrong side! I couldn't see him in time, couldn't react." Roberta was thrust back to that horrible moment. If Luke had ridden his bicycle safely, he'd be alive now.

"See?" Jake said, staying his broom and turning to face her, "That's what I mean. Luke, he don't like rules. If you say white, he says black."

Berta tamped down her temper. She hadn't wanted her post-mortem to become a trial—of Luke or herself. She didn't know what she wanted.

"I just hoped to find out about him. Why people liked to have him around."

Jake swept methodically, up one section and down the next. Roberta hoped he was thinking. She stood to the side, hoping he'd eventually focus on her concerns.

"OK," he said. "I'm done. Come on in, have a Coke or lemonade, or something – coffee?"

She thought she'd be using his ultra-clean restroom in another minute. Reporting takes its toll on one's bladder. If you want someone to talk to you, you drink their coffee, lemonade, or beer.

"Lemonade sounds great! Thanks!" she said, following him in.

"Luke was a unusual fella," Jake began as he sat heavily on the stool behind the counter, having dragged out a chair for Roberta. She sat with her knees up, her boot heels hooked on the cross-brace of the chair. She sipped from a paper cup of crushed ice and chemical lemonade and nodded.

Jake looked out the window at the gas pumps. "He seemed like your regular kid with no sense, but he could hear you if you talked. He knew when someone was sad or angry, and he listened. I had trouble, coupla years ago, and Luke would come in here and hang out. There wasn't any of that crap: 'time heals all wounds,' and 'pretty soon you'll find a new lady.'"

Clearly Jake's wife or girlfriend had left—or died, but now was not the time to ask. She nodded. "Most people don't know how to listen. They think they have to give advice."

"You don't want advice then. You just need to know someone…." The words hung, unfinished.

"That you're not alone?" she prompted, after a moment.

"Yeah. We're none of us s'posed to live solo. Like you. Don't you got no boyfriend?"

Roberta flinched, but she knew the first rule of intimacy: to get something, give something. Secrets are bartered. She took a breath.

"I had a boyfriend. When I decided to come up here, he said he'd visit, but he didn't. The long-distance thing didn't work for him."

"Tough," Jake said. "Folks would say he wasn't a keeper, anyhow. But it hurts, anyhow, don't it?"

She nodded, surprised that this man could make such a perceptive comment.

"So why did you come up here, where no one can find you?"

She had been wondering that, too.

"I got sick of The City," she said, finally, referring to San Francisco. "It was intense. Too many people, too much noise and dirt. Panhandlers. I couldn't afford to live in a nice neighborhood and grunge stopped being romantic. It was depressing."

"I went there once," Jake said. "Couldn't stand it."

"I got sick of the urban lifestyle," Roberta continued. "When some friends of mine moved to Humboldt, I came to visit them and fell in love with the place. I loved that it was far from everything and was clean." She reflected for a moment, then said, "maybe I fell in love with their life. I wanted to be them."

She'd been returning from a cozy dinner at Cyndi and Jeff's when she'd encountered the black-clad cyclist, Luke.

Jake nodded. "So, how do you like it here, so far?"

"Aside from killing your friend, I like it fine," she said.

A car pulled up to the gas pump; in a minute Jake would be occupied. "Thanks for your time, Jake. And for the lemonade."

"Nice talkin' to you, lady. Don't be a stranger."

Roberta tried to work. Each day she got up at dawn, filled and started her coffee maker, and made a fire in the wood-stove. This little redwood house on the edge of the village had been charming that summer afternoon when she'd first seen it, but now the darkness of the redwoods made it dank and cold. She stared at the cursor blinking on the blank screen of her computer. Sometimes she filled time by tweaking pages she'd written weeks ago. The deadline for the manuscript, circled in red on the wall calendar, crept closer, but she couldn't write the crucial concluding pages. The timing of her trouble was truly awful; she mourned the wreck of her sports car, the loss of productive time, the possible failure of a project – but she'd killed a man.

The highway patrol had told her she was not at fault, her neighbors had concurred. But her heart still beat heavily: "Guilty, guilty, guilty."

This chilly morning she'd accomplished nothing; there was no work to take a break from. She took her bag of laundry to the four-machine laundromat, which also housed a rack of videos, a freezer of pizzas, and a one-chair barber/beauty salon. When her jeans and tee-shirts were sloshing in suds, she felt someone watching her.

The square-built woman's face was wide, brown, and seamed. She might have been carved from redwood burl. Roberta could hardly tear her eyes away from the three startling black lines, 111, tattooed on her chin, the mark of a respected Karuk woman. She wore a stiff white shirt and an ancient blue corduroy skirt. Her thin, dark hair was tied back with colored string.

Roberta nodded shyly, wanting to bow with respect but not knowing how.

"You the lady wants to know about Luke?" the woman asked.

"I need to know. I killed him." Roberta returned the woman's level gaze. "Are you Mary?"

The woman nodded. She gestured to the plastic chair next to hers.

Roberta sat. "Thank you," she said.

The woman was silent for a long moment. She spread thick, gnarled fingers over her knees.

"He was broken, like a fallen bird," she said at last. "His soul was broken."

"I met him once," Roberta said, "but I didn't really see him."

"He didn't want to be seen."

"Do you know why?"

They watched the clothes tumbling in the washing machine's round eye.

"He was hurt," the old woman said. "The part that was broke didn't want us to see the part that was whole, the good part."

"Some people saw it, like Dottie and Jake."

"It takes time to see that part. You didn't have time to see."

"I didn't take time to see, and I killed him."

Roberta's hands clenched. The pain had grown larger and sharper each day, each hour, expanding to fill her, not shrinking, as they said it would. She would never be part of anything. Separate, alien, she would always be city-bound, even in the forest.

"He was a sorrow eater, and it was time for him to pass the sorrow on. To you."

"What is a sorrow eater?" Roberta asked with dread.

"One who takes the sorrow of other people into himself. Takes it from them, lets them live. Without him, sorrow would sit in their stomach like a rock, and keep them from living their life. Eating so much sorrow weighs the sorrow eater down, and then he passes it to someone else. Your car killed him because he was ready to throw away all that sorrow."

Roberta's heart pounded as though she'd run up the mountain.

"You don't have to die, Sorrow Eater," the Indian woman said. "You are smart. You can open your heart, take the sorrow, and turn it into something else. Dorothy told me you make stories. You write for magazines and books. So, tell stories: take the sorrow, drain the poison from it, give it to people in stories."

Roberta was starting to follow the woman's rhythmic speech. The healing trickle of words flowed over and through her, but she didn't understand their full meaning. She listened intently.

"You know our baskets?" the woman asked.

"Karuk baskets? They are wonderful!"

"Not basket caps like you saw in Miss Dorothy's diner. I mean work baskets. We make one kind for gathering acorns, another for straining acorn flour. Another for cooking. People cannot eat bitter acorns. We use baskets to leach acid from acorn flour to make food." The woman's voice was scratchy with age, but strong.

Roberta nodded. She'd seen work baskets in the Clarke Museum in Eureka. People's lives had depended on baskets like these.

"We gather acorns. Then we remove the husks, grind the meat into flour, spread the flour in the basket, and pour warm water through it. When the acid is out, leached into the ground, we cook the flour with hot rocks in cooking baskets and eat it like soup. It's plain, rich food."

She continued after a moment, seeing that Roberta grasped the laborious process of making acorn porridge.

"Luke had a good heart, but he wasn't smart. Drink made him stupid. To eat sorrow and live, you must leach acid from it. You can make food of it -- not sweet, but strength-giving."

The woman got slowly to her feet and went to the door. "Be a sorrow eater, but be smarter than Luke — don't gather sorrow to keep it. Weave pain into beauty, like a basket. Then when we think of Luke, his life and his death will not be wasted. His sadness should be poured into the ground like acid, but we should keep the kindness that was in him."

Roberta parked the car in the bare spot in front of her redwood cabin. She walked past her little house into the forest. Game trails meandered and crossed one another, leading nowhere in particular. Brushing past huckleberry vines and blackberry brambles, she walked uphill under redwoods and tan oaks, the kind of oaks the Indians had used for their food, but here growing spindly in the redwoods' shade. The people had found stouter oaks growing on other, sunnier hillsides.

Once the native people had traveled in search of food. They had fished the streams, gathered shellfish on the ocean shore, and roamed inland to find oaks growing stout and heavy with acorns. They didn't sit in one place, wishing for food to drop into their baskets.

She felt herself coming alive again, feeling her muscles straining after sitting for weeks, hunched in her cabin like a snail. Her lungs expanded. The narrow game trails cut between bushes and vines, climbing steeply. She wanted to work against the topography and pretend that no one had been here before her. Finally, she achieved a ridge-top overlooking a series of folds of earth that had been pushing each other up for millennia. The valleys were filled with pearly fog and cloud; the ridges marched toward the coast until they descended into the marine layer. This landscape was a gathering basket full of stories.

Author's Note

A two inch item in the local newspaper said a driver had struck a cyclist on a rainy back road, killing him. I had previously learned something about the Karuk art of basket making. Telling this tale, the images came together in a way that surprised me. I invented the concept of the sorrow eater to fill a narrative requirement, but I believe its emotional truth. Also, I believe that whether telling stories or making something physical, like a basket, art is a human necessity..

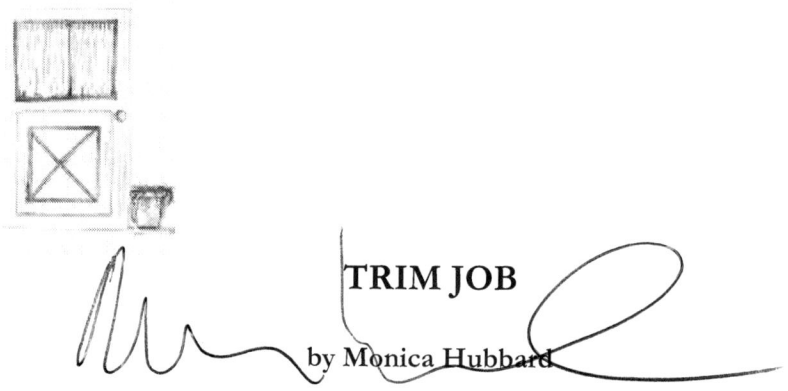

TRIM JOB

by Monica Hubbard

The rain was never going to stop. Mariel looked out the window for five seconds that could have been an hour, and sighed. This job was never going to stop. Things had been going ok, out in the hills, until this morning when Sam, the property owner and majority partner, had shown up with three more workers.

"This is Jenna, Suzy, and Babs." He said. "Ladies, Mariel."

After a round of hellos, all four of the women had sat down to get to work. Suzy, a narrow-faced girl who had brown hair ratted into dreadlocks whipped out an mp3 player with attached speakers and cued up some reggae. Mariel had hoped that the playlist would have some variation, but so far, six hours later, they were still listening to reggae. Babs seemed ok, she hadn't said more than the bare minimum the whole time they had been there, just bobbed her curly brown head in time with the music as she clipped. Jenna, however, had not shut up. Mariel preferred to work in her own little bubble of silence; listening to the rain, going into a fugue state where her scissors seemed to snip along of their own accord, eating up the pounds plant by plant, and Jenna's yakking was severely getting on her nerves. That, however, was not the biggest problem with Jenna.

As soon as she had sat down, Jenna had stripped off her shirt, exclaiming with a grin, "I always trim topless! It keeps my clothes smelling good. I hope nobody minds."

Sam had smiled. "Nope," he said, "nobody minds at all."

Mariel minded, but she was in no position to complain. If the dumb bitch wanted to get itchy, sticky, nasty leaf all over her tits, that was her business; but Mariel kind of had a crush on Sam's partner Johnny, and she didn't need this bimbo distracting him when he showed up.

Really, though, she didn't know why she bothered caring for someone who was basically her jailer. She had met Johnny at a seriously low point in her life, and while she was grateful for his help, she was not totally thrilled with her current situation.

Mariel had run from a bad boyfriend in Eureka, but had only made it as far as Fortuna when her car crapped out. She had left it on the side of the highway, grabbed her purse and her big four cell mag light, and walked out on a road through fields of cattle and bison, past the dump, until she had made it to the Comfort Inn. All of her clothes, her favorite stuffed animals, her cell phone, and her grandmother's costume jewelry were still up in the house in Eureka, but sometimes, you just have to go, right? Right, she thought, shaking her head. Sometimes you just have to get the hell out.

Anyway, on her third day of walking aimlessly around Fortuna, nursing her bruises, she met Johnny as he was having a smoke outside of the Oriental Buffet.

"Can I bum one?" Mariel asked.

"Sure, hon," said Johnny. "How's your night going?"

"Pretty shitty," she said, inhaling gratefully. "You?"

"Another day, another dollar."

"I wish," she said, dryly.

"You looking for work?"

"I'm looking to get the hell out of Humboldt, but I'm maxed out, so, yeah, I guess I'm looking for work."

"You do much snipping?"

"Yeah, sometimes. My ex had a four lighter, and I used to help him every few months."

"Well, we got about 500 plants to get through, so I guess we could use some help. Regular rates, plus we'll feed you."

"When do you want me?"

"How about first thing tomorrow?"

"No funky stuff, right?"

"Nah, baby. You'll be fine."

She had believed him, and really, she had been fine. She was just a little creeped out the first few days. The drive out here had taken so long, and after Myer's Flat, she hadn't recognized anything. The last hour or so had been all on pitted dirt tracks, and she hadn't seen any promising houses, or people, on the way. If she had even seen a dog lolling around, she would have felt easier about the whole thing, but nope, no life at all. Well, at least no civilized life.

When, ultimately, they crested a ridge and stopped, Mariel had been delighted that the little cabin had all of the outer trappings of a comfortable place to stay. The wrap-around porch had a stunning view of the rolling, tree covered hills, and four blue Adirondack chairs with matching footstools from which to enjoy it. There was an extensive, cluttered vegetable garden, and no outhouse in sight. A sign, Mariel figured, of indoor plumbing in her immediate future.

Johnny had leaped easily up and over the four wide steps leading up to the porch, and fiddled open the padlock which was the first sign of this being anything other than a charming cabin in the back-country. When the door swung open, the heady, damp, grassy smell of drying marijuana wafted out and formed a wall of odor that Mariel felt as though she had to push through in order to enter the house.

Once inside, the charming country-ness of the spot fell away to reveal the property for what it really was, an agricultural processing station designed only to coddle the bottom line, not to comfort any human beings. The picturesque chairs from the porch gave way to ratty camp chairs in camouflage print, the lightbulbs were bare, and there was a single, folding, card table sitting in a clearing in the front of the room, right by the door. Fishing line had been used to form a grid suspended from the ceiling, and everywhere Mariel looked, the biggest weed plants she had ever seen hung upside down in rows. The foliage was so thick, she could not see all the way to the back wall, and she realized she would have to fight her way past many of the plants to make it over to the hallway door on the right which beckoned to her with sweet promises of plumbing.

Behind her, Johnny cleared his throat.

"Be sure to put the bungee back on the trash outside after you use it. Helps keep the animals out. The rooms in the back are full up, too. I have a sleeping bag for you, but there are no beds. There might be a couch back there somewhere, but it's buried for the time being. I hope you don't mind sleeping a little rough."

"I don't really have much of a choice, do I?" Mariel said with a little laugh. "If it's not too cold, I'll probably sleep outside for the air. Get some good stars out here, huh?"

"Yeah, if you're lucky. This far into the fall, we get a lot of rain."

Yeah, thought Mariel. Don't we all.

She wondered why they had so much work left to do, and only one person, her, apparently, to do it. From what she had heard, as soon as they harvested, most growers had whole groups of people out trimming everything so that they could clean it up and get it dry before any mold set in. That wasn't important, though. What was important was that bathroom. With a shrug, and a deep breath, Mariel pushed her way between the actual wall of the house and the wall of foliage which filled it. The dark green, papery looking leaves were sharp along the edges, and she kept her elbows up by her eyes, hands clasped in her hair, to protect her face as she made her way around the room. Each plant reached from just under the ceiling almost to the floor, and as she brushed past them, they rustled. It was hard to tell, as they were cut down and drying, but she guessed that, when alive, each plant must have measured at least five feet in circumference, and six feet in height. This was a whole world different from the little three-foot hydro plants she used to help trim, back in her other life, and, not for the first time, Mariel wondered what she had gotten herself into.

The bathroom, finally, was scummy but adequate, and turned out to be the only room in the house where enough of the walls were visible to see the peeling, indistinct wallpaper. She poked into the other rooms--none of them had doors--and saw that Johnny was right. Every space in the house that wasn't wall or floor was filled with drying plant. From her vantage point of the hallway, Mariel could see that the main room contained an alcove which should have been a kitchen, but it had been gutted, and was nothing but more weed.

Suddenly, she felt like the miller's beautiful daughter in the story of Rumpelstiltskin, required to spin a room full of straw into gold within three nights, or else be executed.

By the time she made it back up to the front, Johnny had been out to the truck, and had laid out supplies by the card table. He piled a large cooler, a sleeping bag, and a grocery sack on the floor, and put another grocery bag on the table. Mariel poked in this bag and found a large bottle of rubbing alcohol, a couple of plastic cups and about ten pairs of the sharp, spring-loaded scissors that were ostensibly for sewing, but were sold county-wide for the the use of trimming weed. Knowing what was expected, she poured out an inch of rubbing alcohol into one of the cups, and added four pairs of the scissors, blades down, ready for work. As she trimmed along, she would switch between the scissors; when one got too gummy, back into the cup it would go, and the next would come out, get a quick wipe, and be clean and ready for work.

"Do you have a rag?"

Johnny saw her gesture to the scissors.

"No," he said, grinning. "Just use your pants."

No way, thought Mariel, turning back to the table. They're my only pair.

His eyes, a cross between hazel and yellow, blinked slowly, watching the girl. He could see her clearly as she crossed the porch, and then all but the top of her tousled brown hair was obstructed by a slight rise in the land as she descended the stairs. Soon, he knew, her narrow, pale face and wide hips would come into clear view, as she made her way closer to his hiding place just beyond the tree line. He could smell her now. As she drew near, he could feel the blood pulsing through her, calling to him. He took in a long, slow, intoxicating breath, and settled into a slightly more comfortable position, one that would allow him to watch both her approach, and her temporary escape.

By the time the other girls arrived, a week later, Mariel had cleared out one of the back bedrooms completely, and gotten a start on the other one. She still hadn't found a couch, but had been quite comfortable sleeping out on the porch. It was covered, and the sleeping bag was a nice, arctic weight mummy bag, so the constant rain didn't bother her. Every morning and evening, she had gotten in the habit of taking a long walk out along the edge of the forest. Her sneakers were unrecognizable now, because of the mud, but it was a small sacrifice. She needed a chance to stretch out, un-kink her back and neck from the hours upon hours of sitting hunched in a camp chair, forearms resting on a card table, cleaning the plants. Each one she cut up into its individual stalks before stripping off the big water leaves with her hand. Then, branch by branch, bud by bud, she worked her way from the bottom up, gently pulling each bud away from the stem, and using the points of her scissors to clip out the leaves sprouting from between the fat, juicy, crystal-encrusted calyx formations that formed the flower of the marijuana plant.

After the first hour or so, she was inured to the smell, but even so, days later, she would sometimes give one of the buds a gentle squeeze and let its perfume wash over her. After about three days, she stopped noticing the deep aches in her hands and forearms, and didn't bother scratching at the scrapes and welts she collected anywhere flesh was exposed to the leaves and stems. She didn't smoke any of it. Johnny, before he shrugged at the bag of groceries and hopped into his truck, said that she could smoke her fill of the little stuff, but she wanted to work fast, so had kept her head as clear as she could, considering how much THC she was probably absorbing through her skin. Besides, he hadn't given her a pipe or a lighter, so unless she wanted to eat it, it would all just go into the bag.

One or other of the boys had come every evening to weigh up what she had finished, and bring her more food. The first time Sam had come up with Johnny, Mariel embarrassed herself, because the boys were in a hurry, and she didn't have the opportunity to draw Johnny aside. She was forced to call to him from the porch.

"Um. Wait!"

"What?" he said, hanging his head and arm out the window of the truck as she walked over.

"I need you to get me some, uh, tampons."

"Ok," he said, with an even look. "Any brand?"

"OB regulars, since you're asking. But anything will work if you just want to grab without looking."

Sam poked his head over. "Don't worry, Mary, I do this shit for my wife all the time. I got you."

"Thanks." As she stepped aside to avoid the mud flying up from the tires of the pickup she said, "Mariel. My name is Mariel." The white tailgate was the only reply.

Neither Sam nor Johnny had given her any indication that they wanted her to be working faster, or that there was some sort of deadline, so she was confused and resentful that they brought up these other girls. She had really gotten into a rhythm that allowed her to work fast and not think too much about her problems or the future. Life did not go beyond the next plant or a sandwich, and the rain was going to keep falling, so she could handle this life. These other people, though, cluttered things.

The second day they were here, Jenna, the topless wonder, kept up her prattle for eight straight hours before something she said caught Mariel's attention.

"I hope we can get paid for this shit before those guys catch up to Sam."

"Huh?" said Mariel. "Who do you mean?"

Jenna, Suzy, and Babs sent around a panicked look, and, for a breath, Jenna was actually silent.

"Actually, Mariel," said Babs, in her sweet, baby-girl voice. "Sam and Johnny..."

"Nothing!" said Jenna, jumping in. "Just drop it, ok?"

Mariel just shrugged, and bent her head back to her work, but that evening, after her walk and sandwich, instead of getting in her bag and enjoying the night air, she went back to the table and continued working. She wanted to get this job done, and be shut of this whole situation.

Soon, the chattering from the now cleared room where the girls had set up camp fell silent, and Mariel was able to pretend, once again, that she was the only living creature up here on the top of this mountain. She worked to the steady drip of the rain and the snicking of her scissors, moving now, almost of their own accord, as she twirled each bud gently on its stem so as to get all of the leaves without breaking it off. She liked to trim up a whole plant before she cut off the buds into the bag. It helped her keep track, and just seemed neater somehow.

For days now he had watched her, waiting for his need to overcome his caution. He was leery of the men in the truck, uninterested in the loud women, and too afraid of the house to approach her as she lay vulnerable on the porch every night. These were his woods, though, and every day she came closer, taunting him with her sad eyes and hot blood. He was frustrated, but would wait, and watch, a little longer.

The aborted conversation with the girls worried her. She hadn't actually seen any money yet, although the guys had been careful to make a running tally, which she kept, of the pounds she had completed. They were going to pay her $200 per pound, and so far, she had been working fast and finishing right around two pounds a day. Rarely, that was all off of one plant; most days she got through two or three of the smaller ones. After tonight, she figured they would owe her almost $4,000. She did not like the thought that there might be a problem getting that money, and as her hands worked, her mind worried at the problem, spiraling through explanations and possibilities, until she could no longer tell which seemed paranoid, which seemed logical.

Maybe, she thought, this was not really their grow, and they had brought in the girls to make sure everything was cleared out before the rightful owners came back. Maybe Sam's wife was jealous, and was going to send in men to finish the job, so that her man would not be entranced by some hippie chick and leave her. Maybe the feds were watching them. Mariel couldn't know, but doubted that Jenna would have the inside track with the feds.

Mariel remembered a newspaper article she had read, back in her other life in Eureka, where some grower had had some workers, Mexican nationals, and they had a dispute, and the grower shot and killed one of them, and chased the other one throughout the night so he could kill him too. The guy got away, and the grower was arrested, but what about the dead guy? Would anyone have looked for him, had both men been killed? If that happened to her, who would even notice?

Abruptly, Mariel slammed down her scissors, and stepped out onto the porch. She took in a deep breath through her nose, and tried to clear out the bad thoughts on her long exhale. She needed to focus. She needed to get this job done. There were a lot more plants to get through, and she wanted to do as many of them herself as she could. She needed that money.

A wavering scream out by the treeline snatched her thoughts away from the plants. She felt her face and hands go numb as fear snaked its way down through her throat into a cold, greasy ball in the bottom of her gut. That was a woman. Where had a woman come from, and what were they doing to her? Maybe it was just an animal. Please let it just be an animal, she thought.

Mariel swallowed, or tried to, and closed her eyes so that she could listen to the dark. The only thing she could hear was her heart, tripping out of sequence, scaring her even further. This must be how small mammals die of fear, she thought, their hearts lose the steps, and never can get back into rhythm. Another shriek, this time closer, sent her scurrying back into the house, sitting at the table, wishing the door had a proper lock, one that she could use from the inside, to keep out the bogeyman.

By this time, they had trimmed up enough of the plants to uncover the front window, and earlier that day the girls had moved their little table under it, to catch more of the natural light. That window now seemed to Mariel like the mirror in a birdcage, cruelly throwing back her face, too pale in the harsh light of the bare bulb. She felt stripped and vulnerable. Women might be dying, the night was pressing in, and the sleeping magpies in the other room were no comfort.

"Enough," said Mariel. "Enough."

On her way out the door, she stooped and grabbed her big, heavy flashlight out of her small pile of possessions. Holding it under its bulbous top, like the weapon that it was, she stepped slowly out onto the porch, and paused until her eyes had adjusted to the dark. Then, with a shuddering breath, she walked carefully down the four steps, trying not to step on the creaky parts. Whoever was out there on the ridge, she wanted to catch them by surprise, to take back some of the power she had given away over the long, bad years in Eureka. She would solve this puzzle, she could save this woman, and she would have some revenge, maybe, on the world that had made her afraid. She told herself she did not care; if it was thieves, torturers, rightful owners, feds, whatever, whoever, she would deal with this problem, go back inside, finish the job, get paid, and get the hell out. Mariel had had enough.

She did not turn on the flashlight as it would be a beacon out here on this dark hilltop, and she did not want to find out what kinds of creatures might be attracted. She turned her back on the glow of the house, and took several shaky steps before the rushing of blood in her head deafened her, and she had to stoop with her head between her knees, gulping in air, in order to remain conscious. When she could move again, she stood, face turned upwards, letting tears mingle with the cold rain, run into her ears, and down into the collar of her shirt. When she could hear again, she listened hard but could discern nothing over the sound of the rain hitting the road, the house, the trees, and her face. She thought that she had reached the very edge of her courage, but Mariel surprised herself when she took a step towards the treeline, and then another.

The next morning, Jenna and Suzy awoke to the sound of Babs, shrieking and crying. They ran outside in jammies and slippers to find Babs kneeling in the tall grass on the side of the road, shaking and sobbing. Mariel was lying there, face up, clutching her flashlight in both hands, her body ravaged. Something, some animal maybe, had torn into her throat and her soft belly, killing and eating her in the night. A small distance down the road lay a lone sneaker, crusted with dried blood, saliva, and mud. The rain had stopped, finally.

Author's Note

For this story I did my best to bring a flavor of authenticity to a fantastical tale. Any inaccuracies, or potential felonies, are, of course, purely from my imagination. Although she did not give me permission, I would like to thank the real Mariel....I swear, all I took from you was your excellent name.

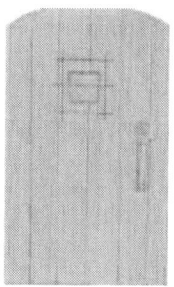

THE ONE YOU DON'T SEE

by Rick Markgraff

A spasm of hunger clamped at her gut. Her silver gray body slid through the ocean with the essence and precision of a machine, pulling in the miles and casting them behind in an everlasting search for fuel. Her great flat head, spanning a meter across from one round dead eye to the other, swayed rhythmically to left and right as it drove through the water.

With each cast, a new taste of water was forced through pores in her head and in the lateral line along her side. Within the pores she sensed pressure changes in the water, as well as chemical changes. The pores also sensed changes in the electrical field surrounding her body like the lines of force in a huge magnet. These detectors provided her with a sensory picture of her surroundings, yet, for almost a week, they had presented no hint of prey.

Finding food now became imperative. She was only days from birthing her young. Her usual hunting range was cleared of food, a trick of El Nino currents known to her only by its effect. She had turned toward the California coast, expanding her range in what was now a desperate search.

Tony MacGuin was sweating heavily from his efforts under the summer sun. His girl, Marla, sitting on a bright green beach towel coordinated to match her bikini, laughed at his efforts but did not offer to help. She appeared content to baste her skin with oil and lean back on her elbows, watching him through designer shades.

"I thought we were going to spend the day together," she grumbled. "How can we be together when you are underwater?"

"This won't take too long," he said. "I just want to try out the suit, and then I'll burn alongside you the rest of the day."

It was difficult to pull the bottom of the wetsuit over his legs. He gripped the nylon-lined material with his big hands, and then tugged it over the red hair of his thick, pale calves, over his swimming trunks, and across his chest to Velcro over the shoulder. When smoothed and stretched, the suit gripped his legs, much like stuffing a sausage. The booties were next, and caused him only a little more effort. He donned the jacket of thick neoprene and pulled the heavy zipper to his neck, then stooped to fasten the beaver tail between his legs. The resistance of the neoprene pulled his arms out straight from his shoulders, so that he assumed the muscle-bound posture of a weight lifter. As soon as his chest and arms were encased, he felt the sun's heat.

While donning the new suit in the comfort of his shady apartment, heat had not been a factor. Now he baked under a merciless sun without the usual onshore breeze, and he still had to pull on the gloves, hood, knife, mask, fins and snorkel. There was, also, lying on the sand in a crumpled heap, the belt with twenty pounds of gray lead he would have to strap on to counter the buoyancy of the suit. He paused for a moment to rest, but the heat of the sun drove him on.

The cool water of Luffenholz Beach, beaded at its margins with flashes of colored swimming suits, beckoned him. The waves were casual today, and the water between the beach and the huge sperm whale shape of Trinidad Head quietly embraced a small fleet of fishing boats at anchor.

Tony saved the hood until there was no other choice, stuffing his light red hair behind the edge, where it had poked out as though trying to escape the heat within. The hood covered his ears and muffled the keening cry of gulls and excited gull squeals of children playing in the waves. After buckling the weight belt around his waist, he picked up the yellow mask and heavy black fins and waded into the sea.

As the water reached his knees, he felt its blissful coolness creep under the suit. He imagined he heard it hiss as it turned to steam. Without grace, he sat down in the water and stretched out a moment, letting a chill wave bubble over his face and into the superheated cavities beneath the suit. The contrast was shocking, but the water soon warmed to a comfortable level, insulating him against the deadly cold outside.

He struggled against the elasticity of the suit to pull on his fins, facing the shore, working by feel because he couldn't bend enough to see his feet. Waves lifted the buoyant suit and, countered by the lead hanging at his butt rolled him backwards and dunked his head under the water with each attempt. Finally, fins in place, he stood, realizing that his work had propelled him into chest-deep water. He was panting from the exertion. He spat into his mask and washed it free of the fog, then pulled it over his face and fitted the snorkel to his mouth. The soft mouthpiece tasted of new rubber and the too-salty flavor of seawater. He exhaled sharply, almost saying the word "too", and felt the water explode from the tip of the snorkel onto his shoulder.

He turned to wave at Marla and found she was not watching, but lay face down, with her bikini top untied. Facing west, he allowed the sea to welcome him into that other world.

More than a mile away, the massive shark had turned to follow the coastline. She sensed a new flavor in the water, a blend of oils and diesel fuel and the secretions from mammals, whose blood always pulsed a sensation of warmth over her mouth and gills. Her hunger drove her forward. Blessed with a small brain in a remarkably sensitive and efficient body, she yet had the capacity for hunger. She sought the pleasure that it gave her, beyond the simple need. Fulfillment of her appetite was more than just survival; she craved the taste and the action of the kill with a lust that was as ancient as life itself. In anticipation, she quickened the pace of her approach.

Tony could hear the fairy-like tinkle of pebbles as the wave action washed them against each other. His ears, surrounded now by water, could hear the heartbeat of the beach with great clarity. He was surprised by the turbidity of the water that blocked his vision, probably caused by wave action against some vein of clay. Six months before, when he was in Monterey diving with the class for his SCUBA certification, the water had been so clear that he felt a sense of vertigo while suspended 70 feet over the ocean floor. Now he could barely see five feet in front of him. He felt claustrophobic. A strand of brown kelp startled him as he passed. He recalled the words of Rene, his dive instructor, as she sat the class in a circle and very solemnly instructed them.

"We never say the 'S' word."

One of the students guessed, "Shark?"

"Ah-ah," she said, emphatically, "We **never** say the 'S' word."

Rene had also said, " If you ever do get in that sort of situation, the best thing to do is head for the bottom and hang around until things clear up. If you can't do that, the only thing left to do is get the hell out of Dodge. Try not to look like an hors d'oeuvre."

He swam harder, hoping the water would clear as he left the sand and silt of the beach area. In his mind, he repeated the mantra, "We never say the 'S' word."

Tony wished that he had practiced more. His calf muscles were beginning to tire from pushing the jet fins through the water. The broad blades were powerful, but they were also taxing his strength. He found himself breathing hard through the snorkel, and decided to rest for a while, floating on the top of the water, the weight belt tugging downward at his hips, looser in the water than it felt on dry land.

As his breathing slowed, he turned to look at the shore, amazed at the distance he had come. He could still see Marla, but only when he rose on the crest of a swell. He took several deep breaths, to hyperventilate his lungs. He tucked his head down and lifted his legs out of the water so their weight drove him toward the bottom. As he descended, he pinched his nose through the soft silicone rubber of the mask, blowing air against his eardrum to equalize the pressure of the water. The turbidity cleared, so that he could now see for a greater distance, but the light was dim. He estimated the bottom at more than thirty feet deep, and leveled off at about twenty. Huge grey boulders loomed into view, and atop one he could see the wall-eyed shape of a large ling cod, well camouflaged as it lay flat on the algae covering the rock.

Unpracticed at holding his breath, he only stayed below for a few moments, looking over the stalks of short kelp and the grayish shells of urchins that covered the patches of sand. There was nothing here of the splendid kelp forest he had seen in the clear water of his certification dive, hundreds of miles south. Disappointed, he surfaced, blowing again into his snorkel to expel the water.

"No matter," he thought. His purpose was to test the new suit, and he was satisfied with its performance. Next time he would rent some tanks and find someone to go out with him. He swam for the shore; face down in the murky water.

The return was more difficult, and Tony realized he was swimming against a mild current. His calves were already aching from moving the fins, and the arches of his feet were cramping. He knew he would be sore from the unusual exercise.

Without warning, his right fin stopped in mid stroke and he was pulled backward through the water for several feet.

"What the ..." Tony yelled past the snorkel in his mouth. His head submerged beneath the water and the snorkel filled. His surprised gasp was met with chilled acrid seawater and he coughed in reflex. The pulling stopped and Tony kicked hard, breaking away and swimming with powerful kicks driven by panic. He pulled the snorkel from his mouth and swam with his face above water, the powerful fins pushing his chest up on plane for several yards. As he swam, he simultaneously coughed, vomited, and tried to pull air into his lungs. The extreme saltiness of the water left an ache in the back of his throat and increased his impulse to gag.

He slowed as reason forced its way above panic. He felt unusual warmth, and realized he had pissed in his new suit. He turned onto his back, still kicking hard, and looked behind him, expecting to see the fin of a shark knifing toward him. There was nothing. Tony reached for the heavy diver's knife strapped to his calf and held it point down. The thick blade calmed him a little, although the thought of stabbing a shark that held him with sharp teeth terrified him. He replaced the snorkel, blew the water from it, and swam again toward the shore.

Now the water was filled with unseen enemies. Tony tried to swim steadily to conserve his flagging energy, but every few strokes he had to turn and look behind him. He could only see a yard or two at best and as he was pushing forward, saw a faint but definite shape glide through the water in front of him. It was light in tone, and seemed huge to Tony. Just how large he couldn't tell, but it swam with ease at a speed much faster than he could manage. He had a long way to go before he reached the safety of the shore.

The hunger was sharp in her as she cut through the silted water. She had felt the thrumming of pressure waves against her lateral line that signaled prey was near. She tasted the chemical stink of fear that threaded through the current and with a massive flick of her tail she sped forward. She circled her prey, moving in closer to it, triangulating position, and finding it without seeing.

Again Tony's kick was interrupted and he flew backwards through the water. The force was unimaginable and his panic returned. He tried to reach his attacker with the knife, but was powerless to do more than flail at the water, a doll being dragged by a child. Tony was released again, several feet beneath the water. Somehow he had kept from inhaling the water through his snorkel, but he was short of breath from his exertion and the struggle to the surface seemed to take an eternity.

He lunged again for the shore, panic still moving his legs as fast as they could go. An incongruous image formed in his head, a cartoon of Donald Duck spinning his webbed feet as he sped across the top of the water. He could not outdistance his attacker, and he knew for certain that he was doomed.

A shape appeared in front of Tony and sped toward him, growing instantly larger. "This is it," he thought, and raised the knife instinctively. Stopping six inches in front of him, the face of a clown puppy peered into his mask and smiled. He saw curious black eyes perched above a cartoon nose that sprouted long bristles.

"Seal," he thought, and relief flooded him. It had been a seal, all along, playing with him as it had, no doubt, with many divers before him. Tony laughed silently and, shaking within his black skin, began the swim again, grateful for the relief from fear.

She was very close now, coming up behind and below her prey. She struck with undeniable force, eyes closed, her great maw opening, nose up and jaws arched forward in a sneer, nearly enveloping it. Warm juices gushed forth as she bit down with powerful muscles, crunching bone and scattering bits of flesh. The force of her strike lifted her above the surface and she crashed down with a great splash of water, her prey limp and broken in her mouth. Beneath the sea, she shook her head, the motion shivering down the length of her body, and then gulped several times until the warm thing was inside her.

Marla lifted her head at the sound of the splash. Something was different that distinguished it from the noise of the surf. She looked in time to see the big tail fin flip in the surf before it disappeared, and knew what it was. Others on the beach did, too.

"Shark!" she heard a man yell, and others took up the call. She reached behind her to tie the strings to her suit top, standing as she did and looking past a knot of swimmers who churned the water, trying to run to the safety of land.

The shark had been close to shore. Where was Tony? She rushed to the edge of the water, and then saw him crawling out of the waves on his hands and knees.

"Tony!" she cried. "Tony!"

She saw him rise to his knees, pull off his mask and tug the hood back from his head as a wave slapped him from behind, moving him forward. He grinned at her and made no effort to get up.

"Tony, get out of the water. There's a shark!"

Tony continued to grin and shook his head. He reached behind him and tugged off the fins, finally standing knee deep and staggering toward her, obviously exhausted. He dumped the gear at her feet, and unbuckled the weight belt.

"There's no shark." Tony laughed. "It's just a seal."

"No, I saw it," she said, "look over there."

Tony followed her pink-nailed finger as it pointed seaward. A large cloud of red stained the tan of the waves. He stared for a moment, his brow knotted in confusion, before his knees buckled beneath him.

Author's Note

Tony is not a Columbus or Magellan, but on his less-distinguished modern level, he is pushing the envelope of his experience. He's only taking a swim, it's true, but the world he enters is as foreign and potentially dangerous as an ancient one. Within his realm, Tony is a novice and a discoverer, if only for a short time.

Much of this story depends on a legend, that of the fearsome Great White Shark that teems beneath the surface, waiting to tear us to shreds. Our knowledge that they are few in number and more selective in their diet does not do much to reduce the fear, especially when visibility is poor. Blame the media, but give healthy respect to the millennia of evolution favoring a small hominid's fear of predators with big teeth. It is a trait made respectable by its successes. It is remarkable in that it also fails to prevent us from calculating, and then taking the risk.

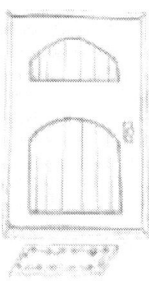

NORTH COAST VAPOR

by Shari Snowden

Pale and silent in the dawn
She hovers over the groves

Lady Bird
Richardson

She spreads her gossamer shawl over the vines to the south

Mendocino
Napa-Sonoma

My sleepy head savors
her chiffon curtain at my window
veiling the early morning rays

At noon,
the mighty sun seethes in from the Trinity
robbing her banks
searing her misty tendrils

I hide my eyes

Frazzled,
she lifts her steamy skirts
and runs for the coast

Author's Note

People grumble about it. I love it. This is my ode to fog with a nod to Richardson Grove. Every tree matters.

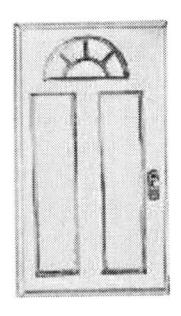

AZARIA

by June Nessler

"Do you think they're guilty?" Helen asked. "That they did something to their kid?" She was slouched in a chair in front of the TV drinking a glass of Chablis. It was a Friday late-afternoon ritual when we would relax with a glass of wine at either her house in Eureka or, today, at my house in Fortuna.

"Even if they didn't, they're in a real mess," I responded. On the screen before us, the attractive, blond news reader had just announced cheerfully that on the 17th of August 1980, Lindy and Michael Chamberlain, a couple in Australia, had taken their nine-week-old daughter Azaria camping near Ayers Rock. They returned from their trip without their baby, much to the consternation of family and law enforcement. The couple said that dingoes, wild dogs, took their baby from their tent.

"Some explanation," jeered Helen. "It just doesn't ring true."

"I can't help but feel sympathy for the parents," I said.

"Oh, come on, Della. You can't tell me you believe their story!"

"Helen, for one thing, we don't know those people. That newsreader was just reading a truncated version of the story…just enough to pull our chains. We don't know the facts."

"I guess you're right," She shook her head and raised her eyes to heaven.

"Before you jump to conclusions about my naiveté," I said, "I want to tell you a story."

She turned to me, eager. "Go ahead."

"It was late spring of 1962. We lived in Arcata at the time. Ben announced that he had a few days off from his duties at the County Hospital in Eureka. He came home early on a Friday and announced that we would take the kids and camp somewhere in the Trinity Alps.

"Ben, do you think that's wise?" I said. "A one-year-old and a three-year-old on such a trek?"

"It's beautiful this time of year," he said. "One of the guys at the hospital said the wild flowers are spectacular right now. We'll take Schultz with us."

"Schultz was our three-year-old black and silver German shepherd. If there's a dog heaven, I know he's there.

"I should have protested more vehemently considering what eventually happened. Honestly, Helen, there are times that I've wondered if I have all my marbles."

"Yeah, you've mentioned that before," Helen replied. "Let me guess. You meekly said OK to the proposal."

"Well, yes. I always took the path of least resistance with Ben. It saved time. He always won in the end anyhow."

"How will we carry everything into the mountains?" I asked.

"Look," said Ben. "I'll plan the things we'll take. We'll keep supplies to a minimum."

"Ben, Jeanie is not quite out of diapers, yet. She'll have to be carried. I can do that, but it means you'll have to carry most of the supplies. Surely you don't expect David, at three, to be of serious help."

"Like I said we'll take a bare minimum of supplies," Ben answered. "Besides it'll only be for one night."

"Well, Helen, we packed efficiently. If anything, Ben is efficient. I guess I've mentioned that before."

"A thousand times."

"At any rate, we got to some place in the Trinity Alps where we could park the car. Ben had a map that one of the docs at the hospital had given him. I couldn't find the place, now, if my life depended on it. At first we hiked up a slope on a narrow gravel road. Ben carried three sleeping bags as well as the dried food and water. I carried Jeanie, her four jars of food, and the dog food as well as her sleeping bag which was a small one. David carried a shovel. And Schultz cavorted around chasing a small animal now and then."

"Sounds like fun," sighed Helen, "You must have been in good shape then."

"I was younger. I used to work out three times each week at the Olympic Club in Eureka. At any rate, Ben was preceding us by about two hundred or so feet. I was busy prodding David who wanted to examine every flower, bug, stone and whatever. You know how little kids are."

"As a matter of fact I don't. Never wanted to know, either."

"The scenery was gorgeous. The mountaintops still had quite a bit of snow. And those guys at the hospital were right. The wild flowers were spectacular. Unfortunately, I was so busy with Schultz and the kids, I didn't have much time to appreciate the natural beauty. In the distance, I saw that Ben was making a right-angle turn off the road. He waved and pointed to where he was going. Then he put a large rock on the road to indicate where we should turn to follow him.

"It took us a while to get to the rock where we were to turn. You have no idea how dismayed I was when I saw that we were to make our way up a steep, rocky slope that must have been an old stream bed. David began to complain that he was hungry. Jeanie must have felt the same way because she was making sounds of discomfort and kicking my lower back. They were not enjoying the trek, and neither was I. We stumbled and crawled up the stream bed which turned out to be steeper than it looked from below. Finally, we reached the place where Ben was waiting for us."

"I've found just the spot where we can set up our camp," he said. "Look! It's beautiful!"

"It was a wide level place on a ridge. Someone else must have camped there for a while some time back because the rocks and other lumpy things had been pushed to the side, making a border around the site on all sides except the downhill one. The air smelled delicious. Ben even had a little fire going. With his help I swung Jeanie in her sling from my back. I could hear a faint fast-flowing rush of a stream, but I didn't see it…until later. I was exhausted, and so was Ben. Schultz and the kids played around the area after we fed them. I could have used a slug of Jim Beam, but he was one of those heavy items we'd left at home."

"What has all this got to do with that news story?" Helen asked impatiently.

"I'm coming to that. Have a bit of patience."

"I've laid out the sleeping bags so that we can be as comfortable as possible," Ben announced. "There's somewhat of a slope, so we'll sleep with our feet toward the downhill side. We'll put David and Jeanie between us. Schultz will sleep wherever he wants to."

"I knew that Schultz would sleep next to Jeanie. She was his favorite human being. At home he was practically her babysitter.

"When the kids were asleep, Ben and I got into our own sleeping bags. I don't remember much after that except that I heard or dreamed Schultz barked and whined several times during the night. I reached over and felt a lump that I thought was Jeanie. I was too exhausted from the day's climb to pay attention to Schultz, who was probably warding off a raccoon or some other small animal. Exhausted, I slept despite the hard ground under me. I wonder now that I didn't at least sit up and find out what was going on with Schultz.

"The next day I woke because the sun was shining directly into my face. Ben and David were snoring away. But there was no Jeanie!"

"Geez! What happened?" asked Helen.

"I tried desperately not to become unglued. In the back of my mind I was thinking that I should stay rational and figure things out. I was screaming."

"Ben! Ben! Jeanie's gone! She's not here! Oh my God! Oh my God!"

"Ben shot up like a rocket. He was out of his sleeping bag in seconds. Somehow it came to me that I should call for Schultz. He would stay with Jeanie wherever she was. So I began to shout for him, but to no avail. He didn't appear as he always did. I could tell that Ben, who always remains calm in an emergency, was verging on some panic. He told me to search downhill, and he would take David and search uphill and the area that surrounded the campsite.

"I began to make my way downhill, tears streaming as I ran from right to left and back again looking for some clue as to the whereabouts of my daughter; at the same time I was yelling for Schultz. To anyone watching, I might have looked like a crazy woman. Still, even in my panic, I could tell that some rocks had been dislodged and some flowers and other low vegetation seemed to be flattened as though trampled. As I proceeded, the sound of that rushing stream became louder. Then I heard whining.

"'Schultz!' I called to him as loud as I could, but he continued to whine. I thought he must be hurt or something. Then I heard a bark coming from the direction of the stream. I stumbled toward it. Then I saw Jeanie's red and white striped sleeping bag. Schultz was on the other side of it. I could see his ears sticking up. I stumbled forward. He was lying in the stream shivering from the icy water draining from snow packs farther up the mountain. He whined and tilted his head the way dogs do, little slivers of ice rushing past and water soaking one side of him. He had wedged himself between a sunken rock outcropping that supported him as he supported the sleeping bag at the edge of the stream bank. Jeanie, thank God, was cuddled in the sleeping bag, sleeping as only babies could through such an ordeal. I don't want to imagine what might have happened if she'd awakened and tried to get out of her sleeping bag. The stream was practically a waterfall that would have easily carried her away to God knows where. I was weak with relief.

"I picked her up and I held her and Schultz against me. I sat there rocking back and forth bawling my eyes out as Schultz licked the tears away. The tension that I had felt eased away, and I felt as relaxed as a rag doll. Later as we ate breakfast I insisted we leave the place and go home. To this day I feel terrible for not having been more alert to Jeanie's, somehow, rolling down that hill...if that's what happened."

"What else could have happened?" asked Helen.

"Helen, it still seems impossible to me that she could have rolled so far downhill. But that's all I can come up with. Of course, you know that if the worst had happened, no one would have believed our flimsy story about Jeanie's simply disappearing during the night." I shuddered, remembering.

"Yeah, I guess the local news people would have been salivating over a juicy story about a local doctor and his wife doing away with their baby."

"You know it," I said. "It's over 15 years since that incident, and I still wake up in a sweat after reliving the nightmare. So, you see, I won't give credence to any sensational story about Lindy Chamberlain and Azaria unless I have all the real facts. And I don't mean the slanted ones such as we've just now heard. I prefer to believe that the Chamberlains are not complicit in their child's disappearance. I cannot imagine that, besides coping with their grief at losing a child, they have to endure the scrutiny of the press and the grilling by law enforcement."

"Yeah, but wild dogs? A little much, I think," Helen replied.

"Who would have believed Ben and me?" I asked. "Can you imagine being camped 100 yards away from that stream, which wasn't even visible from where we were camped, and trying to come up with a theory as to how you no longer have a daughter? We never would have thought of the stream. I still wonder how she got there. I have to think she must have rolled down the hill to it. What would we have told the authorities? Maybe we would have said that a bear or a mountain lion might have carried her off. That would have made some sense to us. But how believable would that have been to everyone else?"

Helen said, "Well, I agree it was a terrible experience for you. But I would have believed you."

"Then you'd have been in the minority, I'm sure. But, think of Azaria's parents. We have no idea how their case will all turn out. The negative publicity that the media will inflict on Lindy and Michael Chamberlain almost insures a guilty verdict."

"Ironic how dogs figure into both stories," she murmured.

I thought about her remark. "Yes, there is real irony here if the Chamberlain story of Azaria holds up."

In 1982 Lindy Chamberlain, Azaria's mother, was tried and found guilty of murdering her daughter. She was sentenced to life in prison. Her husband Michael Chamberlain was convicted as an accessory after the fact and given a suspended sentence (!?). In 1988, Lindy was exonerated and officially pardoned when, along with other exculpatory evidence, Azaria's clothing was found in a dingo lair. Lindy had spent six years in prison.

Books, movies, plays, TV miniseries, songs, and even an opera about the tragedy have been produced.

Author's Note

This is a true story about both Jeanie and Azaria. However, all names except those of the Chamberlain family have been changed. Schultz continued to be Jeanie's baby-sitter, and all he ever charged was food and love. And there was always plenty of both for him.

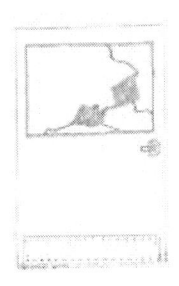

SHE'S ALIVE

by Shari Snowden

"Maybe I should wear something nerdy to court," said Susan, as she watched the woman at the next table gulp down a strawberry smoothie and blot her lips. Her tailored jacket and sleek wool skirt were at odds with the free-spirited lunch crowd at Wildberries.

Troy followed Susan's eyes toward the stranger. "Your hair would clash with an outfit like that."

Susan touched her hair and frowned. "It was just a thought."

"Are you nervous?" Troy asked.

"Yes."

"You'll be fine. Just tell the truth, exactly what you saw. Are you going to finish your sandwich?"

"No. I'm going to change my testimony. I mean, I haven't testified yet but when I do I'm not going to say I saw my cousin that day."

"Why? Is someone threatening you?" Troy sat forward, his forehead creased, eyebrows coming together.

"It's nothing like that. I'm just saying I believe Nora Davenport is innocent."

Troy settled back in his chair, his eyebrows raised. "Come on, Susan. If you saw her there why would you lie about it now?"

"I can't tell the truth. I can't."

"That's a weird thing to say. Why can't you?"

"I made a big deal out of insisting I saw my cousin at Nora's on the day she disappeared, along with Nora's own daughter. I just want you to be prepared. People are going to question my integrity."

"So what is it you're not telling me?"

"Do you want the rest of my sandwich?"

"Susan?"

"You'll think I'm nuts."

"You are a nut, but so what? I like you that way." He smiled and waited for a reply, but Susan only cut the remainder of her sandwich into cubes and moved them around on her plate.

Troy glanced at his watch. "Look, Sue, I've got to go to class. I have a lab in twenty minutes." He stood up, leaning toward Susan and tapping his ample bicep. "If someone is threatening you, I'll take care of it."

"Wait, Troy, please sit down. I'll tell you what happened but you have to promise you won't tell anyone."

Troy looked out the window in the direction of HSU. He shrugged his shoulders and slipped back into his chair.

"Swear, okay?" Susan insisted.

"Here, pass me your knife, I'll swear a blood oath." He reached over and picked up a plastic knife from Susan's plate, holding it against his wrist.

"Be serious, Troy. This is a life and death matter."

"You're right, I'm sorry." He returned the knife to Susan's plate and scooped up the rest of her sandwich. "Go ahead, tell me everything."

Jane Hazelton stood by her hundred-year-old window and watched through ruffled sheers as the young woman approached. She had worried that Susan would be late, or perhaps she wouldn't come at all. But here she was on the front step, ten minutes early.

"So nice of you to come, Susan."

"Thanks for having me, Ms. Hazelton."

"You favor your grandmother."

"Yes, I've been told."

"Please, come in."

The girl was tall and pretty but she had tortured her hair into dreadlocks, reminding Jane of the ghastly beehives of her own college days. "Your grandmother and I met in our freshman year. We did a lot of homework together in this house."

"My grandma loved your house. I've always wanted to see it, especially now that I'm changing my major to Building Design and Construction."

Jane was relieved by her enthusiasm for touring the house. She'd been concerned that Susan would be put off by last month's events. Her young cousin had disappeared from the house next door.

Jane said, "It's a little dusty in here. Seems like the renovation work is never done, but we are happy with the work so far."

"Did you say you did the work yourself?" Susan asked.

"George and I, you remember my husband? We did much of the work ourselves. Of course we couldn't restore everything to the exact year. It was built in nineteen and two."

"The woodwork is beautiful."

"We took three coats of paint off the crown moldings and sanded and re-stained the bannisters. But the wainscoting is new, as close to the original as we could find."

"And the glass?"

"Mostly original. We found a local company to copy and replace the missing panes. And please call me Jane; we're both grown-ups now, despite the age difference."

Susan smiled, "Okay, Jane. But my Grandma always called you Hazel."

"Yes, I was called Hazel at school, *Witch* Hazel, by my detractors. Behind my back, of course. They were afraid I'd cast a spell on them."

Susan hid a smile but her nose crinkled.

"It's okay to laugh."

"You sounded so serious."

"Well, I hated being called Witch Hazel as a child, but by the time I was in high school I thought it was cool to be witchy. I always made myself the finest costume for Halloween. I'm not sure they allow children to dress up at school nowadays."

"I saw you on the Victorian stroll in Ferndale last year. Did you make your dress?"

"Oh, yes, I love the promenade. I made a plaid taffeta, with a green cape and bonnet." Jane inclined her head toward the stairs. "Come on, I'll show you."

Jane made sure the costume showing and house tour were completed by 3:15. She led Susan back to the kitchen.

"I wish I could offer you a proper tea. I used to love to bake homemade treats for my guests but these days I don't do much entertaining. There, on the counter, is a package of Thin Mints. Help yourself if you'd like a treat."

"No, thanks. I've cut way down on sugar. I could go for a glass of water, if you don't mind."

"Our tap water is from a well. It's quite pure, no nasty chlorine. Pour yourself a glass and come out to the patio."

The sun slivered through the tall redwood boughs, reminding Jane why she loved the north coast. It was the kind of day she loved to be outdoors. She saw that the patio chairs were facing toward Nora Davenport's back yard. "Look, over there at the edge of the lawn. They're drawn by the clover. It's what I call honey clover. The deer love it."

"There's another one." Susan smiled as a second fawn stepped out of the trees. "They're so cute and fuzzy. Looks like they're starting to shed their winter coats."

"It's just now 3:30." Jane looked over at the house next door and nodded. "You were at Nora's house on the day the girls disappeared, weren't you?"

"Yes, I was. Did you know that Andrina Hoffs is my cousin?" asked Susan.

"Yes, I thought so," said Jane.

"She's my second cousin, only ten years old."

"Yes, and Katy is Nora's daughter. I don't mean this unkindly, Susan, but they've been holding Nora in jail for nearly a month now. You don't really believe that she would do anything to hurt your little cousin or Katy, her own child?"

"No, of course not. Nora and I were friends before all this happened. But when I go to court, I have to tell the truth. I did see my cousin Andrina at her house on the day she went missing. I didn't actually see Katy."

"You know, Susan, this is a very quiet street. Few cars come this way. I saw you drive by earlier that day."

"That's right. Nora's car was not in the driveway so I turned around and drove back to town. You don't think I…"

"Then you must have seen the van."

"The van?" Susan paused to think. "You're right, I did see a van. I remember it now. It was white, wasn't it? White, with no side windows. Does Detective Peters know about this van?"

"I haven't been able to reach him. Will you call him, Susan? I'm afraid he thinks I'm an old fussbudget."

"I'll call him right now. This could be important. "Susan reached into her purse, a large velvet-brocade bag. She stirred her hand in a circular motion and pulled out a wallet, a brush, a cosmetic bag, tissues, and a mini-notebook. "I must have left it somewhere. Can I use your phone?"

"Yes, of course, it's there next to the cupboard."

Susan took a card from her wallet and went to the phone. "I'm not getting a dial tone."

"I've had some trouble with my line since that last big storm," Jane replied.

Susan sat down and placed the card back into her wallet. "I should be going. I'll call him as soon as I get to a phone." She lifted her glass for a last sip of water but suspended the motion halfway to her lips. The deer were gone from yard next door but as she watched, a little girl walked out of the redwood grove and made her way across the lawn. Susan banged her glass down, splashing water over the patio table.

"Oh, Jane, look, there she is. I thought the worst, I thought…"

Susan leaped up and ran to the edge of the porch. "Andrina?"

The girl disappeared into Nora Davenport's house. Susan stepped off the porch and ran to Nora's back door. She knocked on the glass and waited, but there was no answer. She ran around to the front of the house, but reappeared soon after and hurried back to Jane.

"Oh, Jane, I can hardly believe it. Andrina is back. She's okay," Susan said excitedly. "She must have gone out the front, I couldn't see where she went. Maybe Katy is back too."

Jane kept still.

"Didn't you see her? Come with me, let's go find her." Susan said urgently, holding her hand out to Jane.

Jane took her hand but stayed seated. "You'd better sit down, Susan."

"What's wrong? Is it Katy? Has something happened to Katy?" Susan sat on the edge of her seat, impatient, keeping her eyes on the house next door.

Jane said, "The girls are still missing. Both girls."

Susan's face showed her confusion. She looked from Jane to the house next door and back again. "But I just saw Andrina. Didn't you see her?" She raised her palms in a questioning gesture. "Jane?"

Jane wanted to ease Susan's bewilderment but thought it best to let her come to a conclusion on her own. "I'm sorry, Susan. The girls are still missing."

Moments later, a brief flicker lit Susan's eyes. She shook her head as though in protest. She stood slowly, backing from the table, arms extended, as though pushing something away. She turned toward the door and as she quickened her pace, she heard what sounded like a chuckle. She looked back over her shoulder in time to see Jane Hazelton's lips go from a curl to a frown.

Jane was not at home. Susan had watched her duck into the Rain All Day Bookstore and figured that she might be there for a while. She drove through town, then south to twisty Crab Hill Road. It had been a week since she had toured Jane's house. She drove slowly past the tall gables and wide verandah. Today, she would visit the house next door, Nora Davenport's tiny Craftsman-style cottage. She parked next to a field overgrown with wild blackberry bushes. There were no other houses on this end of the street and no one was in sight. Even so, she closed her car door quietly, scanned all four directions, and moved stealthily toward Nora's front door. She carried a sack containing a hammer and masking tape. She would not be turned away by locked doors or windows.

Susan was fairly certain no one was in the house but she knocked on the front door just in case. She tried the knob, and the door was locked as she expected. She moved to the window on the south side and was prepared to tape the glass and break it with her hammer. To her surprise, the window was open a crack. She wondered if an open window could be a vindicating factor if she were arrested for trespass or breaking and entering. She would have asked for permission to enter, but with Nora in jail, she did not know whom to ask. More importantly, she didn't want anyone else around; this was something she had to do on her own.

She lifted the screen and set it aside. With a little effort, she opened the window far enough to squeeze through.

The room was dark and smelled of must where the rain had soaked the carpet. She quickly pushed back the curtain to let the light through and found herself in Nora's bedroom. A dark splatter discolored the wall and window ledge where she had slid through but she did not stop to consider what it could mean. She stepped around an ominous stain on the carpet and hurried through the hallway into the kitchen. The light was faint, but she found her way to the sliding glass door and drew back the vertical blind. She left the door closed despite the stench in the kitchen. She had seen Andrina through the glass that day and she wanted everything to be exactly as it was.

She looked at her watch. Ten minutes to go.

On the day the girls disappeared, she stopped by to pick up the Girl Scout Cookies she had promised to buy from Nora's daughter, Katy. She chose a box of Samoas for Troy and a box of Do-Si-Dos for herself. When Nora handed her the boxes from atop the refrigerator, she said that Katy was late, and she was worried. Susan suggested that Katy may have stopped to see a friend, but Nora was certain she would have come home first. As Susan left the house at 3:30, she saw Andrina walking across the back lawn. She waved to her but didn't stay to speak. She assumed that the two girls, best friends, were together, and all was well.

3:25 PM. Five more minutes.

Nora's kitchen chairs were askew and dishes were scattered and out of place. The police, she guessed, had tossed things around during their search. Susan stepped back and stood next to a large ceramic pot by the front door, the exact spot she had stood on that day.

No one had taken out the garbage. It reeked. Maybe she should stay and clean it up. Or maybe it was something else. She'd heard that ghosts carried a putrid scent. And if Andrina came right through the glass door in three minutes, would the room suddenly turn cold? Such bizarre thoughts. She was getting spooked, losing her nerve. Ghosts are just spirits, Susan told herself, just spirits who are waiting to transcend to a higher level. Breathe, Susan. Just breathe

One minute to go. Seconds now.

Andrina emerged from the redwood grove, and waltzed across the lawn as though mortal. Fascinated, more than fearful, Susan waited.

The girl slipped through the glass door as though it was invisible. She circled Susan on a cool breeze, smiling and singing her name. A rush of love and compassion passed between them, filling their hearts. The wind picked up speed and spun them along, compelling them toward the wall.

Susan sensed Andrina speaking, not in words, but her meaning was clear. Don't be afraid. The wind changed direction and turned icy cold. They were blown back against the wall by a gale force surge. As the lights dimmed, a huge face loomed above their heads, like a creature in a 3-D movie. The face was rough-skinned but not remarkable except for its fiendish eyes. Susan's impulse was to flee but she was held fast by the force of the wind. At her side, the little girl slipped her arms around Susan's shoulders, comforting her. This is not right, Susan thought, Andrina is only ten, I should be the one to comfort her.

The wind crossed itself, shifted course, and the enormous face cracked into fragments and shrunk away.

Andrina's screams, as piercing as sirens, filled the air and careened off the walls. At the same time, she felt the girl's quiet presence surrounding her, protecting her. Susan trembled and her heart raced, the only movements her body could perform while held in place by thin air in this strange distorted reality.

The screams ceased abruptly as the air temperature rose and the face of Katy Davenport, eyes dripping tears, floated above their heads. She raised her hand and motioned for them to follow. Still bound by the wind, Susan could not move or speak but her mind formed the questions, *Where are you, Katy? How can I help you?* Katy's image swirled and faded as an icy gust burst through the room, and the vicious brute returned. He scooped Katy up and carried her off to a waiting van, leaving Susan in a futile struggle with a raging tempest.

Susan felt a nudge from Andrina, bidding her to be calm. She closed her eyes, accepting that she had no power or influence in this mysterious realm. As she relaxed, the wind ebbed and whispered gently with the warmth of a Chinook. A kiss brushed her cheek, and she sensed that Andrina was drifting away. Susan opened her eyes. She was alone.

It was raining when they left Arcata. From the top of Crab Hill Road, it looked as though the storm was following them south. Susan parked directly in front of Jane's house.

"Are you sure she's home?" asked Troy. "The place looks deserted."

"Jane likes to sit on her back porch in the afternoon," said Susan as they climbed the stairs, "but we'll be polite and knock on the front door first."

Troy looked at his watch. "It's not even four o'clock and it's almost dark. I'd want to be indoors today if I were her."

They waited, but there was no answer.

Susan stepped down the stairs and looked back at the house. "Look up, Troy, at the turrets and the vintage stained glass."

Troy looked up. "I see storm clouds gathering above multiple chimneys and pointy things."

"Finials," said Susan.

"Gothic," said Troy. "Creepy."

"Scared?" asked Susan, with a snicker.

"What's so funny? I'm not scared, not at all," said Troy, squaring his shoulders as he looked across the yard at the house next door. "Where exactly did you see…"

"Come on; let's go around to the back," Susan said, leading the way.

Halfway around the verandah, Troy stopped. "You go ahead, Sue. I'm going next door to have a look around. I'll meet you back here in a few minutes."

"Okay, but the front door is locked. Try the window on the far side."

Susan came around to Jane's back porch just in time to see her crossing the lawn.

"Hello, Jane."

"Oh, Susan, I'm so glad you came back. Come in quickly, it's starting to rain."

"I shouldn't have run off the other day. I was being childish," Susan said, as she sat down on a dusty antique wingchair.

"No, you had every right to be afraid. It's a normal reaction."

"I guess that's true for some people but I should have known. I mean, Andrina wasn't my first—I don't like to say ghost—it seems disrespectful. I saw my grandma after she died. I was missing her and she came to my room and hugged me. It just felt natural."

"I'm not surprised," said Jane. "Your grandmother loved you very much. It's unfortunate that people have turned ghosts into sinister characters. An undeserved reputation."

"That's for sure. Most people wouldn't understand. I owe you a big thanks for not letting me swear in court that I'd seen Andrina."

"I didn't mean to frighten you but I couldn't just say out of the clear blue sky, 'Susan, you saw a ghost.' You had to see for yourself. And I owe you a big apology. I didn't mean to laugh as you ran out the door. I don't know what came over me."

"I must have been funny. Jumping up and running off like I'd seen a ghost."

Jane smiled, but it was a sad smile. She said, "I'm sorry about your cousin."

"Thank you," said Susan, "I saw her yesterday. I went back to the house and she showed me what happened. I want to catch this monster who killed her. I called Detective Peters and told him about the van. What else can we do?"

"I knew I could count on you, Susan. You're very much like your grandmother. As for me, I'm afraid I've done all that I can. It's up to you now."

Nora Davenport waited for the guard to let her through to the visiting room. She had mixed feelings about seeing Susan. They had been friends until the girls disappeared. Susan had blamed her, turned against her. She could have refused to see Susan but then she might miss news of the girls. She couldn't take that chance.

The guard nodded and she walked through to the visiting booth. A thick glass separated the inmates from their visitors. Nora saw Susan waiting and pointed to the telephone. Before Susan could say a word, Nora let her anger speak for her. "What the hell are you doing here, Susan?"

"It's okay, Nora. I'm here to help you."

"I thought you were going to testify that I'm a kidnapper and a murderer."

Susan held up her hand. "Hear me out, Nora, I think the DA's case against you is going to fall apart very quickly now."

Nora sat down hesitantly, still not trusting that Susan meant well. "What do you mean?" Then in a softer tone. "How can that be true?"

"It's true. For one thing, I'm not going to testify against you."

"Have they found the girls?" Nora asked, her voice cracking with anguish and hope.

"No, not yet."

Nora brushed at her tears with her sleeve. "Why the change of heart?"

"I honestly thought I saw Andrina at your house that day, but..."

"But what?"

"But I didn't."

Nora intended to find out exactly what she meant. She had been locked up in jail for nearly a month, dying inside, accused of the worst kind of evil, not knowing what had happened to her beloved daughter. Katy was all she had in the world. How could Susan just suddenly change her mind?

"What the hell, Susan?" Nora meant to sound threatening but her voice was choked with tears.

"I didn't mean to hurt you, Nora. I only meant to tell the truth. I'm sorry; I want us to be friends again." Susan held her hand against the glass.

Nora nodded. She believed Susan was sincere but she still wanted an explanation.

Susan said, "I'll tell you all about it, Nora, but first, let's talk about the investigation. Did Detective Peters ask you about the man in the white van?"

"Yes. I know a guy named Bret Jonast who drives a white van but I didn't see him that day."

"I did, though," said Susan.

Nora sat straight up, her eyes wide. "You saw him at my house?"

"Yes, I saw him and so did Jane."

"Jane?"

"Yes, Jane Hazelton, your next door neighbor. She has been very concerned about you and the girls."

Nora dismissed what she said about Jane. She had attended Jane's funeral two months ago, long before the girls disappeared. But this news about Bret Jonast could be the first break in the case. "You saw Bret Jonast *at my house?*"

"Yes, I came by around three, I thought you would be home by then but I didn't see your car."

"I got stuck behind a wreck on Broadway. Go on…"

"So I turned around to go back to town and I saw him pull into your driveway. I mean, I saw a white van pull in. At the time, I didn't know who he was, but Jane said she'd seen him at your house before."

"Oh God, he's got the girls." Nora banged her fist on the table in frustration. "I don't even know where he lives."

"Who is he?" asked Susan.

"We went out a couple of times but I didn't like him. There was something creepy… disturbing…about his eyes. Does Detective Peters know you saw him?"

"Yes, and he's already tracked down a Suddenlink van that was in your neighborhood that afternoon. But he knows the van I saw was not a company van. It was plain white, with no side windows, and we got the license plate. Jane saw Violet Fields yesterday and she helped her remember it."

"Who is Violet Fields?"

"The hypnotist."

"Oh…" said Nora, doubtfully.

"Violet is for real," said Susan.

"Yes, I'm sure she is," said Nora, trying to keep the skepticism out of her voice. "But hold on a minute, Sue."

Nora needed some time to think over what she'd heard. The conversation was getting stranger by the minute. She had seen Jane buried and put flowers on her grave. But on the other hand, Susan's turnabout was truly a blessing, and if the cops were really going after Bret Jonast, and it made sense that he was the one, then she had reason to hope for the first time since her arrest. She would not bother Susan with her doubts.

"Thank you, Susan, thank you so much. I had no idea anyone was on my side. And please, when you see Jane, thank her for me." Nora was not being facetious. In life, Jane had been a good friend and she felt that she was not in a position to reject help from her friends, living or otherwise. Grateful tears slipped down her cheeks. "And thank God there's finally a clue. An actual lead. Bret Jonast, that sorry son-of-a-bitch. I know it was him. They've been wasting their time, questioning me over and over. I thought I was their only suspect. My P.D. has already been talking to me about a plea bargain."

"I don't understand why they were so quick to arrest you. Surely, it wasn't because I said I saw Andrina at your house that day."

"No, there's more to it than that." Nora took a deep breath. "After you left with the cookies, I called around to some of Katy's friends. They'd seen her with Andrina but no one answered at her house. So I thought, if Katy's not home by the time I change my clothes, I'm calling the police. I went to my bedroom to change…" Nora paused. "Are you sure you want to hear this?"

"Yes! What happened?"

"I saw Andrina's sweater on the floor. There was so much blood. Oh, Susan, I'm sorry."

"Please, go on," said Susan, taking a tissue from her pocket.

"I called 911 and asked for an ambulance. When they arrived, I was the only one home and I was standing there holding the sweater. They asked what happened and I showed them the blood. I can't remember what I said. I was in shock. It must have been something crazy because the next thing I knew the police were there and I was arrested."

"It was her fluffy pink sweater," said Susan, blowing her nose. "She's on her way to heaven now."

"What?" Nora's heart bounced off the walls of her chest. "Are the girls dead?"

"She was only ten…" Susan broke down, sobbing.

"Susan!" Nora cried out, drawing the attention of her fellow inmates and a walk-by from the guard. "*Is Katy dead?*"

"No, no, not Katy. It's Andrina, my little cousin. But she told us…" Susan closed her eyes and looked as though she might break down again.

"What do you mean, 'Andrina told you?'" Nora asked anxiously. "You spoke to Andrina?"

"I meant to say Jane. Jane and I…" Susan hesitated again.

"Please, Susan, just tell me." Nora pleaded, holding her breath.

"We have good reason to believe that your Katy is alive."

"She's alive," Nora repeated, allowing herself to exhale. She crossed her arms and hugged herself. She almost smiled. It was the first time she felt like smiling since the day Katy disappeared but she couldn't smile with Susan in such distress. "How do you know?" She asked.

"Okay," said Susan, "I'll tell you everything, but this is just between the two of us."

Nora took a deep breath and sat back to listen. She wished she could jump up and go after Bret Jonast, but she could only wait and pray for her release. She wanted to believe Susan. It was clear that she could not tell the difference between the dead and the living, but so what? Deep in her heart she knew that Katy was alive. Maybe someday she would tell Susan all about Jane's funeral, but not today. Today, Susan brought a glimmer of hope. And at the moment, that was all that mattered.

Author's Note

I love ghost stories but not the kind where all the ghosts are demons. Two out of three of the ghosts I've met were sweet. Just wanted to see if I could give you a little chill or thrill.

My fascination for old houses is shared by my husband, John, and my daughters, Kristy and Ashley. Before our move to the north coast, we lived in a colossal Victorian (custom replica) in Visalia, California. Kristy and her husband, Nick, owned and restored a century-old home in Butte, Montana and they currently live in a vintage Craftsman Bungalow in Erie, Pennsylvania where she studies Building Design and Construction.

ADVENTURES IN BIRDWATCHING HUMBOLDT COUNTY, CALIFORNIA

by Anthony Westkamper

  2011 seems to be a bumper year for egrets in Humboldt County. There are probably three or four times the number I've seen before. They are majestic birds, snowy white, standing near four feet tall on black stilt legs. When in flight they have an impressive wingspan. In my mind they have always personified the word regal. That was until yesterday.

  You can usually see them at Hookton Slough. It is in range of my computer's air card, making it a good place to do some of my required administrative work while sitting in my car. There is a gravel parking lot, a small floating dock, several large Monterey Cypress trees, and a pair of smelly pit toilets housed in one building with a partition wall between them. Each one has its own lockable door.

  Usually the great white wading birds stand at intervals of fifty feet or more away from each other along the edge of the water. Occasionally, you can see one strike with its long slender beak, catching a small fish or other water creature. You seldom see even two of them close together. This day, though, there were fifteen or more in one small group at the bend just up from the parking lot, all about two or three feet from each other. I was enthralled. I wondered at their social structure, and if they had a pecking order. Why would solitary wading hunters gather together in a cluster like that? From what I could see they weren't actively hunting. They weren't actually doing much of anything...until for no apparent reason one did a face first pratfall into the water. I watched as it thrashed wildly in the water, wondering if it might have been attacked from below by a leopard shark or something. Eventually, it regained its feet and waded out of the water. As it gained the bank it struck at the nearest bird with its long yellow bill.

  Taking long strides it stalked up the slope pecking at each bird that came in range as it went. "Don't look at me!" it seemed to be saying.

The Rain All Day Writers

I know they have strange names for various animal groupings: A murder of crows, a pride of lions....Could I have identified the first "Embarrassment of Egrets?"

Birdwatching is an interest I found later in life. Birds give me one more thing to like about being outdoors. I seldom give avian nesting behavior much thought.

I was parked near the toilets in the shade of the cypress trees working through my perpetually delinquent email list. The popping sound of tires on gravel alerted me that another car had arrived. The car was a dingy old Volvo station wagon, the kind hippies drive. It parked at the other end of the lot.

I didn't give it a second thought. Cars come and go from time to time. Eventually though, a young woman got out of the passenger side. She was wearing a knit cap and clothing that looked like several layers of army surplus. The driver's door opened and a young man sporting a scruffy goatee and darker, sharper clothes emerged. I'm not sure if they noticed me sitting in my company car with my laptop on my lap.

The girl made her way past the car and into the nearest potty door. Then the boy made his way past me and into the nearest potty door. This I noticed!

I wasn't watching the clock but they were probably in there together for five or ten minutes. Eventually she emerged, blushing furiously; clutching her hands tightly to her chest, she trotted back to the Volvo. In another minute he emerged and walked jauntily to the car. They kissed once on her side of the car, got in and drove away.

Like I said, I don't usually pay much attention to nesting behavior, but in this case I wondered what inducement the rakish male used to draw the much less showy female to this particular site.

Some years ago, I was loading my dolly with tools behind one of the hospitals I serviced, preparing to enter through the ER doors. This particular day I had to park pretty far downslope since other cars were taking up all the closest spaces. I didn't mind. It gave me a few more seconds outdoors in the open air. To the left of the entrance is a low square box-shaped extension of the stucco wall. The box was a convenient place to sit outside of the Emergency Room for a person waiting for something.

Looking upslope a movement caught my eye. It was a crow's head bobbing intermittently up and down on the other side of the box. I find crows interesting. They are intelligent and have their own ways of doing things. I figured someone must have been eating there and dropped some chips or a fragment of sandwich. Smiling, I loaded up my cart, looking forward to seeing how close I might get to the bird before it flew off. Some of them are pretty brazen and you can get very close.

Closing up the van and starting toward the box I scared out a shiny healthy looking bird. A second later I was shocked to see the most sickly bird I have ever seen jump up, hop a couple of times to gain speed, and then flap its dusty gray wings frantically trying to gain altitude. It was missing all but four or five of the big primary feathers on each wing and sported only three or so tail feathers. Its whole body exuded an air of frailty and sickness. Here and there tufts of gray under-feathers poked out through its lusterless body feathers.

Shaking my head, I continued uphill until I was abreast of their feast. I didn't see remnants of snack food like I'd assumed. What I did see was a slowly expanding puddle of strawberry milkshake pink vomit. The crows hadn't yet gotten all the chunks when I'd scared them from their feast.

Delaying the start of my job, I sought out the highest placed manager I knew and told him what I'd seen. He was grossed out and said he'd get someone on it right away.

Several hours later, when I left, it was still there and the sickly crow was back. The evening ER desk nurse said they'd get someone on it. The next day and the day after that it was still there. I had told everyone I knew about it and each time they concurred that it needed to be addressed immediately and said they would get someone on it right away.

The pink stain persisted until finally, weeks later, the rain washed it away.

I was dragging my feet like a reluctant child knowing that long division awaits inside and the day was so sunny. I searched overhead and found no motivation to go indoors and start work.

The sky was a clear pool-cue-chalk-blue. I noticed a bird making its leisurely way across the sky.

It is hard to tell how far away something is, especially when it is high up in a cloudless sky, but the general shape and the pattern of its wing beats told me this was a gull. They're common and I usually don't give them much attention, but I was dragging my feet so I watched it, envious of its freedom.

Suddenly, out of nowhere a dark object plummeted directly at the sailing bird. It looked like a near miss, and the cannon ball descent was stopped by a pair of immense wide wings. I was amazed by the sheer brute power of the muscles forcing such huge sails against the air at such a velocity. After two groaningly powerful wing beats I noticed the white tail and head. This was a bald eagle! Turning in air it climbed once again. The gull started to dive away, but the eagle folded its wings high over its back and dropped like a stone toward the its victim. Gulls are adept fliers and can soar and sail seemingly effortlessly. I assumed it would be more maneuverable than the much larger bird. I wondered if the eagle was trying to kill the gull for food.

This time the gull was aware of its pursuer, and tried to sheer off at the last second. At my range I couldn't tell how successful it was, but again and again the great raptor wheeled in the air and, using amazing strength, dove on the gull, forcing it ever lower, until I saw it drop its fish. I don't think the fish dropped twenty feet before the eagle had it and was on its way.

This aerial display gave me a whole new appreciation of the power of our chosen national symbol.

Although they were crows, I've got to call them Heckle and Jeckle in homage to the twin magpies of Terrytoons fame. Like their cartoon namesakes they were mischievous and worked as a team. The unfortunate object of their attentions was a single large gull.

"The plane just landed in McKinleyville," my friend behind the counter at FEDEX said, looking at the clock on the wall. "Give it a half an hour."

What to do with half an hour? It comes up from time to time. Not enough time to go anywhere and do anything, but too much to stand there and look stupid for thirty minutes. So, I returned to the company van in the parking lot, got out my cell phone, and started working my way through my voicemail messages.

Movement caught my eye. Directly across the street in the Costco parking lot was a small dark blue pickup truck.

There was a crow on the tailgate and one on top of the cab. Crows are pretty common in Eureka. They were both looking down into the bed of the truck. One squawked and the white head of a gull popped up, beak agape in a threatening manner. The gull extended its wings and, launching itself awkwardly straight up, flapped a few times and landed on the cab of the truck. This displaced the crow that had been there. He hopped down into the bed of the truck, which was where it wanted to be. The truck bed was full of garbage! The gull, with its wings extended, stood on top of the cab and squawked while the crow rooted through the trash, throwing out whatever it didn't like.

The gull screamed and jumped down into the trash again. The crow hopped out and flapped its wings, hovering over the gull. The gull rose to the challenge and the other crow dropped down from the tailgate to the prize. The flying crow circled and landed on the tailgate. Once again the gull ended up squawking on the top of the cab. I'm sure it was wondering what had just happened.

I think either crow alone would have outclassed the sea bird. As it was, I never saw any contact between any of the birds, and working as a tag team the crows got the opportunity to examine all the trash in the back of the truck, throwing out much of it, despite the gull's best efforts at defense.

In the end the crows abandoned the field to the gull. I don't think they gave up because of the gull's exertions, but because they'd determined that whatever delights had been in the trash were exhausted. They left the gull standing in possession of the useless prize. It looked about blankly, squawked several times, and launched itself up and away. Unfortunately, I didn't have time to wait for the truck's owner to return and discover his truck's contents strewn all over the lot and his truck covered with bird droppings.

Once again birdwatching had provided a most excellent half hour's entertainment.

Author's Note

This collection of tiny vignettes are all true, no imagination was necessary at all to recount them, only the work of putting into words that which I've witnessed.

I am not a true birder with a "life list" etc. but I do find them interesting now that I've taken a little time to look for rather than beyond them. My original intent was to show the other stuff I often see when I'm out looking.

A FRIEND IN DEED

by Rick Markgraf

"I just don't like the man!" Walter slammed his fist into an open palm and stalked to his kitchen window. The panes were dark, but reflected the image of a tall man with gray hair and a trimmed silver beard. His features were stern and set by strong emotion.

"Why, Walter. I'm amazed." Jennie moved to his side and slipped her slender hand into his. " I've never known anyone you didn't like. Just this morning, Gregg was telling me you were the most popular in your class at school. No one has as many friends as you. Really, I've never danced so hard or laughed so long in my life. You always throw the best parties." Jennie's hand was moist in his, and her brow and neck were still beaded with sweat from the polka they had danced in the living room. Her red dress sparkled with tiny sequins that winked darkly in the lamplight.

Walter's demeanor softened at her words and he turned his head to her. She was ten years younger than he and a foot shorter. He put his arm around her and hugged her bare shoulder. His rough hands enjoyed the smooth warmth of her skin, and it was nice to feel her beside him. Too bad she was taken, but he felt only mild regret. Her husband, Gregg, had been his best friend since boyhood. She reminded him slightly of his own wife, Dottie, who had died so long ago.

"I should have baked more cookies," Dottie said, bustling into the kitchen and smiling at Jennie and then carrying a tray of canapés back to the room.

"That's a hungry bunch out there." Walter felt an overwhelming sadness at the sight of her.

In the next moment, Walter found himself strangely alone. The room around him was silent and slightly disheveled, with no sign of the partiers. Puzzled, he cast about himself for some evidence of his friend. Then, as though recovering a lost train of thought, he found her again beside him and the noise of laughter floated in from the adjacent room.

"I don't really know why," he continued. "He's a harmless old goat, and a priest of his church, and he is trying to do good. Why does he have to come here? He can't even play chess, but he insists on sitting there every

Wednesday, the whole day through, and falling for the same gambits time and again. I just don't like him at all."

She smiled at him, an open, friendly smile that used up her whole face. There was something to it that just naturally attracted men, including him. It wasn't a seductive smile, or even inviting, but it always compelled him to linger and listen, and to talk. She was not particularly beautiful, as fashion dictates beauty. She was simply interesting. Her phrases, her thoughts, her point of view, were uniquely hers and she had a way of expressing them that assured she would never bore.

"He probably just wants some company," she said. "Must be a lonely job. When you talk to God all the time, it must be nice to have someone your own size to talk to occasionally."

A burst of voices and music accompanied the opening of the kitchen door, which banged against the wall. "Mommy, Cootie's bottle is empty and he keeps waking me up. Can I have some milk for it?" Jennie's gawky 8-year old, Zoey, waved the empty container over her head while rubbing an eye with the other.

"Sure, honey, give it here, and will you please stop calling your brother Cootie? We named him Todd because we like it so much better." She rinsed the bottle briefly under the faucet, then filled it again with milk from the refrigerator

"Cootie fits him better." The girl seemed all legs and arms, like a stick drawing of a person, but when she spoke, her mother's smile graced her elfin face. "I sure hope his diaper can hold all this," she said, as she reentered the party on her way to the bedroom.

Walter laughed. Zoey was a bright kid, and apt to say anything. The boy was the sweet one, though. Just that afternoon, he had crawled onto Walter's lap, removed the spectacles from his ears, and carefully placed them on his own. Walter watched as the toddler peered owl-like through the glasses for a moment, then looked directly at him and grinned. Next he removed Walter's fountain pen from his shirt pocket, then carefully pulled it apart, reassembled it, and clipped it back in place. He threw both arms wide, and leaned forward, falling against Walter's chest and hugging as much of the man as he could gather in. Walter inhaled a rich combination of soap and urine, and lost his heart to the tyke.

But wait. Somewhere, there was also the memory of the tyke as a youth. Brash, blond and handsome, the boy showed virility that Walter himself had lost. How could he be here now, as a babe, when Walter knew him so well as a young man? Walter sat in a rocker, alone again, and pondered the question. He stood and wandered to the window, seeking the view that calmed and sustained him

Below, a wild plum had sprung into bloom like a burst of fireworks reaching for the canyon below. Bees flooded from their box at the edge of the clearing and were humming their sugar song among white blossoms warmed by the afternoon sun. A silver thread of the Eel River gleamed between trees as it curved along its traditional path against the arc of cliffs. Far below, in the depths of the canyon that sheltered the town of Rio Dell, a white church spire gleamed above a mass of tiny buildings, almost indistinguishable one from the other. It housed his nemesis, he knew, and it was nearly time for the battle to begin again.

On Wednesday, as predicted, Walter opened his door to a small ruddy man in black, save for a white cleric's collar. "Oh, it's you," Walter said, and then turned away, leaving the door open.

"Aye, it's me, and who else would it be, then? Shall I invite myself in or will you find some shred of hospitality in your own heart and give me the word?"

"Well, you're here. I guess you might as well come in."

"Ah, yes, I see there was the smallest shred, after all. I hope it didn't hurt."

Walter opened a battered checkerboard and laid it out on a table by the window, then emptied a paper sack of chess pieces onto it. "Did you come here to insult me, or to get beaten again?"

"Both, I say. There's little pleasure in one without the other." He closed the door and reached out to tap Walter's hand, choosing from the two held out to him.

"White," Walter said. "You first. You'll need that bit of luck later. It's a shame to waste it now."

The two men sat at the table, facing each other in silence, and changed their positions little as the day wore on. Sunlight through the window formed a cross on the floor that moved slowly with the hours, sweeping over the boards, as might the hands of a clock across its face.

"I met Jennie Forbes at the store yesterday," The visitor said at last. "She asked after you. Seems she used to come see you, but never found you home." There was no answer, no evidence he had even been heard, and the day continued in silence.

Finally, the last king was tipped and by unspoken mutual consent, both men stood and stretched. The one in black walked toward the door, opened it, and turned, as if to make his farewells.

"I've a question to ask you," Walter said, walking toward the open door.

"What would that be?"

"Why do you torture yourself like this? There's not even the slightest chance you will win at this game. Why come here every Wednesday?"

"It depends on which game you mean," he said. "I might yet win at the one I'm playing, even though I know there's little chance I'll win at the one you're playing."

"Well, I know your game bears little resemblance to the way most people play, but aren't we both playing chess?"

"Walter, I live at the bottom of the only path up the ridge to your cabin. You've lived here for ten years, by yourself, since your wife died. I know for a fact that I'm the only person beside you who has walked that path in years. I don't believe any man should live so much alone, so I come here every week to remind you what it's like to have a human being around."

Walter stood by the door. His face glowed red in the light from the setting sun, and his mouth turned down, his jaw working as though trying to find words for his lips. Finally he spoke. "You've overstayed your welcome. Get out."

"Right then. I'll be back next Wednesday." He walked through the door and closed it before Walter could say more.

Walter turned and found Jennie waiting for him at the kitchen door.

Author's Note

I pondered the question of subtle delusion. There is rarely an awareness of its presence by the victim, who thinks of his own reality as the correct one. The madness of another is easier to believe than your own. Is normal just a majority opinion?

In "A Friend In Deed," I tried to see this from the point of view of a victim. It is the most difficult story I have ever attempted.

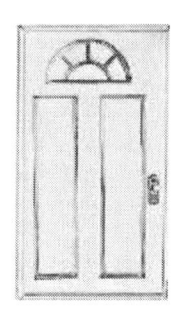

BASED ON ACTUAL EVENTS

by Lisa Baney

Janie asked, "Ready?" Carlisle looked at her, a pleasant expression on his face. He was wearing the warm-up jacket she liked; it blued and electrified his grey eyes.

Just inside the entrance to Winco she hitched a cart out of the line and started down the cavernous aisle. He kept pace with her, looking about himself, relaxed, hands in his pockets. Food shopping with her. "Do we need condensed milk?" she asked. "Look, it's on sale." She glanced at him. He smiled at her.

"Christmas will be so great this year," she said.

Her cell phone rang in the produce section. Carlisle was looking at the late-season avocados. She checked the screen and, heart pounding, answered.

"OK, I'm calling you back," Carlisle said. "What's up?"

"Hi," she said. "Hey, I was thinking, can I take you to lunch? Like...tomorrow? Do you get a break at all?" She pleated her lips. "I can come down there."

There was a pause, typing sounds, sporadic and muffled conversation. "Yeah, you know," he said. "I don't know. Let me call you back."

"Oh. OK," she said. "Good, yeah. Later." She was talking to dead air.

Janie switched off the phone and peered around her, feeling the sudden absence of him. She was, indeed, alone. An ache started up under her ribs.

She finished her shopping, the ache growing in her as she rolled down the aisles, picking out canned beans, pasta, bottled water. She stared at the other shoppers, seeing harmonious bonding in the fact that they were shopping together, and the ache deepened.

At the checkout counter she looked at the smiling, smooth-skinned women on the magazine covers and pulled her mouth into a smirk. "Photoshopped," she muttered, contemptuous.

Next to her came the sound of someone scoffing. She looked up. Carlisle.

"Do men really believe this?" she asked, poking at the image of a coyly nude woman. He smiled cynically.

"I didn't think so. Men of quality, anyway," she said. They shared a look.

They were silent as they bagged the groceries and on the way out Carlisle put out a hand to keep her from walking in front of a clueless driver. She felt a sudden wash of happiness. This man was her best friend.

That evening she busied herself with necessary tasks. The phone was silent. As the night wore on the ache grew, and with it came a kind of distant keening that Janie could feel as a faint thrumming in her inner ear. At 11:00, suddenly almost immobile with fatigue, she dragged herself in to run a bath, lit a candle and switched off the light. She sat back in the steaming water and closed her eyes. "I really need this," she whispered aloud.

There was a movement at the foot of the tub. Carlisle, naked and lithe, slid into the bath with her. She slitted her eyes at him as he squeezed bath oil into his palm, picked up her right foot and began massaging it. He watched her face and matched his movements to the minute changes in her expression, his fingers strong and sure and perfect.

"God," she said, "Oh god."

After a while she stood and he toweled her dry. They got into her bed and she curled up into him, his warm hands on her and his hot kisses pressed against her neck. As they moved together the ache gathered in her, tore open and expanded, and the keening she'd been straining to hear all night grew until it was a savage, snarling roar. Her throat was dry and tight and sore; and she understood: the keening was coming from her.

The next morning Janie stared at her face in the bathroom mirror. Her eyes were swimming in red, the skin under them like soft purple velvet. This couldn't go on; she'd be barking at strangers next.

She walked into the kitchen and sat down at the table, and before she picked up the phone to call Carlisle's work number she took a deep breath. She dialed, the phone rang once and he picked up, snapping, "Yes?"

"It's Janie," she said.

"I'm in the middle of something right now," he said flatly.

"You're never going to call me, are you?" Janie said. She watched the dust in the air above the table move in and out of the sun's gimlet glow.

Silence. It sounded aggrieved.

"Look," he said finally. "We had some great conversation, we're on the same page about a lot of that stuff. But I'm really busy in my life right now."

She caught at her words, struggling, failing, to corral them. "It wasn't just conversation." The words bled from her. "We slept together. You told me stuff."

"OK, yes, we slept together," he hissed, his voice low. She imagined co-workers, straining to hear. Or maybe there weren't. She'd never actually seen where he worked. He could be making this all up, this life of working 18 hours a day and then going home to a silent girlfriend, his emotional life parched, devoid of love, and instead was sitting poolside somewhere with a frosty margarita at his elbow. "It was great, you're great, you're beautiful and sexy and great. But I just don't have time to spend with you." She heard him take a swallow of something. Coffee? Tequila? "If you want to get together every once in a while, fine. Just—leave me alone now."

Janie was silent. She listened to the noise on the line for a beat, two, three.

She hung up.

She stared at the dust motes for a while. There was nothing in her head. Finally she took in another breath and straightened. "It's over," she sighed into the empty room.

There was a faint rustling off in the corner. Janie turned her head. Carlisle was looking at her, his eyes full of mournful yearning.

Hating this, her words coming strangled and harsh, Janie said "You have to go." Instantly, as if jerked by strings, he turned, reached for the doorknob, and went out, closing the back door quietly behind himself.

There were several bad days, weeks really, during which Janie forced herself to get up, get herself dressed and in the car and down to the redwoods. She hiked for hours most days, breathed the sweet, heavy air and let herself get chilled through. The trees were like mothers, or aunts, looking down on her and offering profound, leafy advice. She strained to hear them. Afterwards she turned the car's heater on high and drove through the short, inky twilight to her empty house and slept like a woman in a coma.

The ache was fearsome for a while but then, bit by bit, shrank until she could fit it into the rusty metal box on the closet floor, the box that was always underfoot. With the toe of her hiking boot one afternoon she nudged the box into the back of her closet, way back in the corner, behind the 80s-era floor-length evening gown with the fake, glued-on purple sequins.

The week before Christmas she walked into Ramone's in Old Town for a *breve latte*, a treat for having finished her Christmas shopping early. The windows were streaked with condensation, the place packed and overheated, the sound of conversation and foam-making so cacophonous she had almost to shout her order. There was one small, crumb-strewn table free at the back; without looking around she rushed to it, brushed it off, settled herself, and with a sigh began to read the newspaper someone had left.

"Excuse me," came a male voice. She looked up into and then gaped at one of the most intelligent pairs of deep brown eyes to ever meet hers. "Would you mind if I shared your table? There are no other seats and I'm totally wiped out."

The eyes belonged to a Mathew McConaughey lookalike, only more mature and interesting-looking. Mathew McConaughey's older, way less narcissistic, doctorate-seeking, mutt-owning, once-married-but-long-single, new-to-the-area brother in a well-worn sweater.

They talked, and he was comfortable and funny. After an hour he offered her his phone number. "I know this is hopelessly cliché," he said, "but if you're into it I'd love to see you again. Maybe for a hike in the woods sometime?"

She left Ramone's in a haze of cautious well-being. The day had gone dark and it was pouring rain and foggy at the same time. Janie drove distractedly, her thoughts behind her, so that the red light at the busy Wabash intersection took her by surprise and she had to step hard on the brakes. She immediately looked in her rear-view mirror and pressed her head back into the seat's neck rest.

Aloud, she said, "Habit. I was rear-ended in 1994 and got whip-lashed."

And then, "Dammit!"

She closed her eyes briefly and then forced herself to look over to the passenger seat. For the first time in weeks Carlisle was there, gazing at her, his face open and warm. In his lap was the metal box. Her metal box.

"What are you doing here?" she said, weariness on her suddenly like a weighted veil.

With a movement of his hand—as if she couldn't already clearly see it there in his lap—Carlisle indicated the box.

"And what are you doing with that?" The light was still red, this interminable traffic light, the ruddiness staining Carlisle's pleasant face.

"It's not going to work," Carlisle said. She looked at him, astonished, fear blooming in her.

"You're talking," she said. "Why are you talking?"

"He'll be just like all the others." He looked appealingly at her. As she watched his eager face bright with anticipation, he moved his hand to the lid and unlatched the crusted clasp. She caught her breath, batting at her panic. In a moment the lid would be open and that fucking ache would fill the car's tiny space and her and everything, and she would be lost, quite possibly die, or at the very least want to, right here in this ten-year-old car on this wet street in this cold, streaming winter night.

Or...not.

Janie looked into Carlisle's shining eyes, considering. She could take that thing, that creaky, discolored, immortal old piece of junk, the thing her mother had passed down to her and her mother to her before that and all the women back and back and back in her mother-line, take that thing and lift the lid and let the ache come slithering out, welcome it, clear the space it needed to coil up and settle in, live with it for a while, have long conversations over tea or brandy with it. Get to really know it. She could do that.

"Give me that," she snapped, grabbing the box out of his unresisting hands. "And get the hell out of my car. Now."

Without hesitation Carlisle turned, opened the door, and stepped out into the dark and the weather and the frenzied traffic. Behind him the door snicked shut and she was alone.

Janie looked down at the box in her lap, red as freshly-shed blood with the light outside. It was smaller than she'd thought, and lighter; with her fingertips she could feel a faint tracery of intricate etching on its surfaces. It seemed...weary to her, somehow, ancient, and, oddly, priceless. Looking at it she was seized with a sudden eagerness to open it right that very moment; but the light changed, and, caught in the middle of the massed, slow-moving traffic, Janie took her foot off the brake and started for home, one hand firm and protective on the lid of the box.

Author's Note

I wrote this story to vanquish one small, pesky ghost. It turns out there were a bunch of ghosts, and that I couldn't possibly hope to get rid of them all. And anyway what would I do without them?

TALIA

by June Nessler

"What will you do?" he asked, as she pulled on her skirt.

Talia pursed her lips and looked at the ceiling. At last she said, "I'll take something."

"No." He took a pad from his pocket and wrote something on it. She took it and saw that it was a telephone number. "There's help."

She shrugged. A sudden wave of depression washed over her.

He put his arm around her as though sensing her anguish. "You'll do fine." He patted her shoulder. "Just call that number." He walked her to the door. "You'll do fine," he repeated before he closed the door behind her.

The rain had stopped. Not even the smell of the dampened eucalyptus and redwood trees lifted her spirits as they would have under happier circumstances. She gazed at the grey, heavy overcast sky that pressed down on her, making her pace heavy and slow. Suddenly the clouds parted and spectacular sun rays forced their way through the opening. The doorway to heaven, she thought. Was it a sign of a happy time to come? She used to believe in such signs, but no longer. She trod along, finally arriving at her car that she'd taken the precaution to park in the Riverwalk Lodge parking lot. No sense in taking a chance that someone would deduce anything from where she'd been. She got into her car and simply sat and let the depression envelop her. Talia Santini, she thought, why did you behave so stupidly? She closed her eyes rested her head on the steering wheel, emotionally exhausted. As usual, at vulnerable moments such as now, she began to relive events that had brought her to this pass.

"Ta-li-a!" It was so dark. She thought she recognized the voice. Then there were others. They were the boys from the school. Jocks! "Tal-i-a." Singsong-y now. They were coming closer. She was glad she was in her car. Well, it wasn't really her car. It belonged to her foster parents. They allowed her to drive now and then.

"Tal-i-a, Tal-i-a." A knock on the window. "Come on, Talia, we're havin' a blast." There were five of them. The tallest one, T.J., held a bottle of something up to the window and beckoned to her. She had always been beguiled by T.J.'s handsome face and great body.

Mesmerized, she got out of the car. Later she would always wonder why she had done this. The boys surrounded her and sang , "Tal-i-a, Tal-i-a." They began tentatively touching her, tickling her. She giggled. Suddenly, one of them grabbed her breast and made sucking sounds. One of them punched her in the face. Then she was on the ground, pressed by a body on top of her, hands ripping her skirt and panties from her. One of them held her shoulders down. She screamed, but only once before a vile-smelling rag was shoved into her mouth. She was unable to move. First one, T.J., she guessed, raped her to the rhythmic chanting of the others; then the next one, and the next. When all five had finished, one of them kicked her ribs and her face a few times. "Thanks for the good time, bitch!" he said and then they were gone, whooping and laughing. She would always remember their laughter. She struggled to pull the rag from her mouth, every move bringing stabs of pain to her groin and rib cage. She lay in the dark alley behind Ron's Club. It was hard for her to breathe, and she wondered if her ribs were broken. Unable to move or make a noise above a weak moan, she would have lain there all night had not one of the workers at the club decided to empty some trash. She remembered the shock on his face and his shout for somebody to call an ambulance and the police. The police were there in minutes as the station was only a block away.

"Miss?" a gentle male voice said. "Hang in there. We've called an ambulance. Can you tell us what happened?"

It was impossible for her to articulate through swollen lips and aching jaw. The young officer said, "That's OK. Looks like someone really did a number on you."

Talia raised her forearm and held up five fingers. At the time she wanted to yell the names of all the boys who had done this to her. But the EMT's were there doing things, one of which was to inject her with something that took away the pain and made her feel dreamy.

They rushed her to Redwood Memorial Hospital emergency room. She was transferred to an examining table and a soothing warm blanket was put over her. Someone asked, "She's comatose?"

"I've sedated her."

She felt something cold on her chest. A voice said, "Steady heartbeat. She'll be OK for now. Where's the damned rape kit?"

Talia didn't remember anything more. When she awoke in the hospital room she heard someone say, "Ah, she's awake." It was the voice of Mama Sarah, her foster mother. "Talia, how do you feel?"

Her mouth felt like she'd eaten gravel. "Water," she croaked. Mama Sarah held a straw to her lips.

"Talia, what happened last night?" It was Joseph, her foster dad.

"Joe, this is not the time to go into that." Mama Sarah, again.

Joseph growled, "Who did this, Talia?"

"Joe." Another warning from Mama Sarah.

Talia tried to push the unusually tight blanket from herself, but Mama Sarah told her that she shouldn't pull at the bandages. "The nurse told me that the bandages support some fractured ribs."

Talia nodded, not surprised at the rib diagnosis. She feigned sleep, hoping that Mama Sarah and Joseph would leave. She wanted to think.

There was a tapping at the window. Startled, Talia raised her head from the steering wheel. A police officer was peering into the car. "You OK, Miss?"

"Yes, I'm fine." She lowered the window. He looked familiar. "I must have fallen asleep."

"Hey, Miss Santini, is it? You look a lot different from when I first met you. How are you?" He must have seen the questioning look. "It was about a month ago when I found you behind Ron's Club. Remember?"

Talia looked at him closely. She remembered. He had spoken the first kind words to her as she lay in pain. Flustered, she said, "You were very kind. Thank you."

"Just doin' my job." He was quiet a beat, smiled and said, "Hey, that's what police guys say on TV." He studied her. "I think about you. Any memory, yet, of what happened that night?"

Talia shook her head slowly.

He peered at her. "The bruises have faded a lot," he observed. "How about the ribs?"

"Oh, I'll be fine," Talia replied. "I have a little pain now and then."

"And now, here you are."

"Here I am," Talia chirped. "I must have fallen asleep. Honestly, all I did was rest my head on the steering wheel and next thing I know you're here."

"Dennis," he said, "My name's Dennis."

"Talia," she said. "Well, I guess I better get home. I've given my parents enough worry to last a lifetime."

"Well, then, take care, Talia," said Dennis. He waited until her car left the parking lot before he got into his Crown Victoria and continued his rounds.

She drove slowly. She thought of Miss Baragar, her school counselor, to whom she had related the whole story, omitting the names of her assailants. She was afraid Miss B. would report them to the authorities, making things even worse. She had to talk to someone, though.

After listening to Talia, Miss B. had put her arm around her. "You've endured some terrible things in your short life, Talia." She put her hands on the girl's shoulders, "but you are a remarkable girl in that you've managed to overcome very harsh obstacles." Then she looked at her sternly. "You'll find out in life that it is not the experience but how you handle it that shows what you are made of; and so far, you've proved to be made of very strong stuff."

Talia, who had had little sleep as a result of her worry, said, "I think I may be pregnant. I've never felt so nauseated and tired."

"You're tired because you've allowed yourself to become depressed," said Miss B.

"I feel so defeated. Everything seemed to be going right, and then I do something stupid."

"Stupid?" said Miss B.

"I shouldn't have gotten out of the car."

"But you did. That's all over. You can't do anything about the past. Forget it."

"Forget it?" Talia thumped her abdomen with her fists. "I'll have a reminder the rest of my life!"

Miss B said, "You don't know for sure if you're pregnant. I'm going to give you the phone number of a gynecologist whom I know. Make an appointment with him as soon as possible."

"Will he call my parents?"

"No, I'll call him and tell him the circumstances." Miss B. studied Talia whose despondency seemed to filled the room like an enormous gray cloud. "Talia, why do you think you're to blame?" she asked

"I know I am," Talia said.

"You're not. What those boys did to you is a crime against you...a felony…. Why aren't you angry? Why aren't you enraged?"

"Angry?" The truth was that she felt humiliated and, somehow, dirty. Angry? Yes, she supposed she felt a little anger… at herself.

"Stop feeling sorry for yourself, Talia. This is no time to feel depressed and guilty. It's time to take action. You should want revenge for what they did to you. Rage is good. It throws you into action. Make that appointment with the doctor so that you know your circumstances. Never, never hide from your problems. Do you understand?"

"I …I think so," stammered Talia, but she wondered how she'd pull herself out of the funk she was in.

She arrived at the house of Joseph and Mama Sarah in time to help get dinner. She was their only foster kid at the moment. Mama Sarah asked how school went that day.

"Oh, fine," she replied. "I stayed to complete a paper that I have to hand in tomorrow. And thanks for letting me drive the car today. It helped with the field trip transportation." Instead, she had gone to the gynecologist that Miss B. had recommended. She hated lying to her foster parents. They had taken her in four years ago when she was rescued from her abusive father who had made her a surrogate sexual partner after her mother died. Mama Sarah and Joseph had never said an unkind word to her. They had insisted that she stay home from school until she healed. Joseph allowed her to use his computer, and she was able to get her assignments off the school website. She would stay with Mama Sarah and Joseph until she graduated from high school, class of 2009, only a few months away.

She felt in her pocket for the slip of paper that contained the phone number. The smell of cooking brought on a wave of nausea. She excused herself and went to her bedroom. The last thing she wanted was Mama Sarah trying to minister to her and finding out about everything. Feeling a little better, she returned to the kitchen.

That night she lay in bed planning the next day. She wondered if she had the courage to do what had to be done.

Talia knew that T.J. almost always had lunch at Bob's Footlongs near the school. At noon she waited just around the corner of the school at Twelfth and "L" Streets. He was alone, ears plugged, listening to his iPod. He didn't see her until she stood in front of him, blocking his way. He had avoided her for weeks. Later, she realized, if she hadn't been so worried about herself, she would have considered this a delicious moment.

"Hello, TJ," she said. "Haven't had a chance to talk to you for quite some time. I'd begun to think you were avoiding me."

He unplugged his ears. "Gee, Talia," he said. "The guys and I wondered how you were." He was actually smirking.

"Oh, I'll bet you were," she said. "I've been waiting to tell you all something important." She drew nearer to him as though to impart a confidence. "I've been informed that there was a lot of DNA evidence collected when I was in the hospital that night. You remember that night, don't you? Remember? They can preserve DNA for years in an evidence locker. Did you know that?"

TJ began to fidget. He moved to pass her, but she blocked his progress. Clearly nervous, he said, "Hey, listen, it was consensual. You got out of the car and joined us," his voice high and wavering.

Talia found it hard not to slam him in the face with the books she was carrying. "I didn't ask to be raped, nor did I consent to be beaten," she hissed. "The police wanted to know who'd hurt me so badly. But I told them I couldn't remember what happened."

T.J.'s shoulders relaxed and he let out a breath of relief.

She continued calmly, "Who knows when I'll suddenly remember?" She watched him squirm. "And with that in mind, there are few things I want you to do, understand?"

She watched his expression change to alarm.

"Are you talkin' fuckin' blackmail?" he screeched. "It's a crime to blackmail somebody!"

"Yeah?" said Talia. "Well then, go call the cops." His loss of composure was enjoyable despite her persistent nausea. She had the upper hand, now, and would have it for the rest of his sorry life. The big jock; the rich kid; the kid with the acceptance to Harvard, which now depended on her silence. She had never in her life felt such power. What a rush! Miss B. was right. Rage helped her cope. Rage made her powerful. "It's all over for you," she continued, "if I ever hear that you mistreated another girl. In fact, if there is even a hint that you and your neanderthal friends didn't take no for an answer from any girl, not just from this school, but anywhere, I'll finish your careers when my repressed memory surfaces. Get it, bastard? This is only the beginning of the many, many, many demands I'm going to make on you and your pals."

T.J. actually looked frightened.

"And that's not all," she said.

His eyes widened.

"There have been rumors going around; nasty, nasty rumors that you and your friends have started about me. I suppose you were trying to cover your asses just in case. So, I'm an easy lay, am I? Well, I want those rumors squelched. I want my reputation to be snowy white within two weeks."

"How am I going to do that?" T.J. whined.

Talia put her index finger to her head, squinted into the distance, "Oooh, I feel a repressed memory surfacing. Yes, in back of Ron's Club ....all that DNA and all!"

"OK, OK," squawked T.J.

"I'm in line to be valedictorian," said Talia. "I've worked hard for it. Now my not-so-great reputation, thanks to you and your knuckle-dragging pals, might color the decision. You all had better hope that I walk across that stage in June to accept that honor. Go to church and pray fervently for it because, if I'm overlooked...well, my memories may become quite vivid, and I'll have to talk about them."

She turned to go, but then said, "Keep in mind those three letters, D-N-A." And she left him.

She ate her lunch alone in her home room. She felt much better now. But she was bluffing in her conversation with T.J. She only knew what she had learned about DNA through TV's CSI. And Law and Order SVU had taught her that revealing her assailants' names to the police would only result in her being grilled by some expensive attorney their families would hire, while she had to make do with an overworked deputy D.A. The odds were that she'd end up with, at very best, a sullied character that might affect her future opportunities. She had a full scholarship to Humboldt State University and she intended to take advantage of it.

Later that afternoon during a study hall she left the school, found a working pay phone on Main Street, and punched in the number her doctor had given her. After the second ring, she heard, "Women's Health and Family Planning Clinic."

Talia, trying to think what to say, did not respond until after the voice repeated the message.

"I need to talk to someone," She blurted. "I've been raped, and I'm pregnant."

She was given an appointment for the next day along with an address in Eureka. She would ask Joseph if she could have the car "to do a little shopping." After some thought she decided that today she would catch the Humboldt Transit Bus to Eureka to find out about the Women's Health and Family Planning Clinic.

It was a longish walk from the bus stop in Eureka to the address she'd been given. At first she thought she had come to the wrong place. There were a lot of people milling about. Some were chanting and carrying signs that portrayed bloody fetuses as well as slogans which she was too far away to decipher. She watched a woman struggle through the crowd that were purposely blocking her entrance into the building. Talia asked a woman standing near her, "What is going on? Who are these people?"

"They are the Pro-Life people. They think that every woman who enters that building is going in to have an abortion," said an elderly woman.

Another woman said bitterly, "I'm due to go in there to have my annual pelvic exam. I'll have to elbow my way through these people because I can't afford to go anywhere else."

"I'm going to put off my mammogram. I'm not going through that crowd," said another and she hurried away.

So, thought Talia, this is what is in store for me tomorrow. A KVIQ news van was setting up photographic equipment. The activity seemed to excite the crowd who held their banners toward the camera lens. This alarmed her. All she needed was for Mama Sarah and Joseph to see her on the Evening News. How would she explain being here? She ducked out of sight behind a high escalonia hedge. She was glad that she had come, though. She was not about to miss tomorrow's appointment because of a few people with nothing better to do than to try to control her life. As she returned to the bus stop, she planned how she would handle them.

The next day, bright and sunny, was not a day to be dressed in a heavy, gray hoody with the drawstring drawn tight about her face. She put on large sun glasses. Hardly recognizing her own reflection in the mirror, she chuckled. She looked like the Unibomber! She removed the disguise. She would pull off at the College of the Redwoods parking lot and don it before entering Eureka.

The crowd was still at the clinic. Some were on their knees praying with the lobotomized expression that's supposed to convey piety. Others looked at Talia angrily as she approached the entrance. Didn't these people have jobs to go to? She elbowed her way forcefully through the throng. An angry young woman got in her face yelling "Baby Killer!" spewing spittle. Talia had been marshaling saliva of her own since she left her car. She rounded her lips and blew, showering those nearest to her. Finished, she shouted, "Better wash up. I'm HIV positive!" The crowd backed away in a single move; some that had been nearest to her rushed away, probably to wash up. She entered the building easily.

The receptionist, who had been watching the activity through the window, said, "What just happened out there?"

"You just have to understand crowd control," Talia replied. "Do I sign in or something?"

"Oh, you must be Talia," the receptionist said. "And right on time, too." She handed Talia a clipboard with some sheets to fill out and said, "Dr. Toensing will be with you soon."

Dr. Annabelle Toensing was an amiable, motherly woman. She made Talia feel at ease. She said, "The urine test is positive for pregnancy. I've received the necessary information from your gynecologist in Fortuna."

"Not more than four weeks," said Talia, "pregnant, that is."

"Correct," said Dr. Toensing. "Three or four weeks into the first trimester makes the procedure simpler."

And so it was over. When she left the building, the fearful crowd, recognizing her as the woman with AIDS, parted, allowing her to pass. As she walked to her car, Talia waited for the feeling of guilt that rumor said would assail her. But all she felt was relief. The world was opening up to her. Life was suddenly exciting! She could make plans! She thought of those rays of sunlight that had appeared for an instant when the dark clouds parted the day before. She took a deep breath and smiled. She was in charge, a winner, and best of all, she knew it.

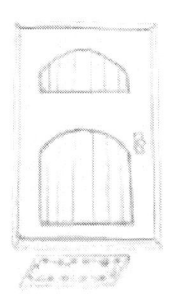

ENTER "Y" FOR YES

by Anthony Westkamper

Mama's biography was written in the creases and stains on her raincoat. The frayed tag over the inside pocket no longer proclaimed an exclusive New York clothier's name in gold thread. The elbows had long since turned baggy, stretched out by years of use. Four of its six buttons still matched, and the original hue under the collar was now several shades darker than the faded exposed material. Despite all that time had taken away, its quality endured, resisting the day's cold North Coast drizzle.

"Come, Runt." The woman's sharp features were matched by a crisp New England accent as she called out for her dog. Mama's dark, active, beady eyes searched the path, and concern drew fine lines around her mouth and between her eyebrows.
"Don't tell me you found a dead fish to roll in again, or a skunk," she said to herself. "If you did you're sleeping in the shed until the stink wears off you." In contrast to the bedraggled coat she pulled a cheap modern waterproof hot pink scarf over her close-cropped gray hair. She called her hairstyle a utility cut. "Like they give poodles that aren't being shown," she would explain with a wry grin.
Patting herself down she verified all buttons buttoned, keys in left coat pocket, a can of bear mace in the right, and her pocket camera in the gun pocket. Blue jeans and well used hiking boots finished off her "look" for the day. Smiling, she thought to herself that there wasn't a single restaurant in the county where her get up would be out of place.
Runt was a black flash bounding up the driveway, full of puppyish enthusiasm for the rain, the adventure, and the attention. "Come on, girl, let's see what the world of rural living looks like today." They set off at a brisk pace.

The breeder had given Runt away with the proviso that she be spayed as soon as the vet said it would be okay. "She's too small for a standard Lab. We've got to maintain standards. She'll make a good pet, but you can't ever show her."

"I've had enough show dogs. She's just going to be a companion." Mama said as she scratched behind the dog's ear with coarse ridged fingernails turned to talons by years of exposure to harsh photographic chemicals. Her hideous nails were all part of the syndrome that gave her voice its distinctive raspiness, and had pushed her off of her throne in the world of high fashion photography. In turn, the loss of her six figure income had pushed her out of New York City.

She'd met Carl a few months after fleeing the east coast and her toxic career. He was second fiddle in the Technology Department at The College of the Redwoods. They'd found a house in the woods and moved in together and set up a life. Then one morning Mama woke up in a bed soaked with urine. Reflexively, rage and disgust prodded her to push on Carl and he'd rolled out of the bed like a rag doll hitting the floor with a solid thump. He hadn't stirred. Out of bed and around to Carl's inert form on the floor she searched for a pulse. He was alive and breathing on his own. She called 911. Carl had suffered a massive stroke in his sleep. EEG readings indicated brain activity. He could chew a little and swallow if food was fed to him. The neurologists told her he would never move on his own again nor speak. They worked out the one blink for yes, two for no, thing and then left the two of them to cope.

She rested the body of the camera on the ground aiming upwards at a tall slender mushroom. The angled viewfinder let her see the image from an awkward squatting position. She peered closely at the numbers automatically generated by the camera. "Hmmm, not really enough light down here on the forest floor; either I'll get motion, shallow field, or the flash will burn it out." As her finger started the slow squeeze that would take the shot with minimum shake Runt suddenly galloped up the path to see what Mama had found. The impact sent them both sprawling.

"You stupid bitch!" It was a phrase famous ten years earlier for inspiring terror in fashion models all along the Eastern seaboard. Runt regained her feet instantly. Mama stayed sitting on the saturated ground as frigid water soaked her butt. Narrowing her eyes in fury, she prepared to repeat the words with increased venom. Runt ran forward, licking her owner's face and wiggling in happy abandon. "Damn it dog, now I'm all wet. Get off me, you clumsy cow!" Mama knew Runt didn't understand the words, only the tone, and the vitriol had leaked out of them before they were uttered.

"Look, you stomped all over it. It's ruined. It looked like a skinny model in one of those stupid parasol dresses Ingmar was so fond of foisting off on fashion ignoramuses." Runt didn't understand but liked being talked to.

As the walk proceeded, Runt, having run off most of her puppy energy, stayed close to her mistress. Here and there they stopped as Mama snapped pictures of tiny huckleberry blossoms, and a panoramic series of shots climbing up a lone redwood. Later, after Runt was fed and she'd put Carl's hospital bed into its nighttime configuration so he could sleep, she would boot up her laptop. This was her third attempt at stitching the component shots into a composite of the entire tree. Her previous attempts each had flaws that irritated her professional eye, making her delete the whole thing.

In the morning as she spoon fed Carl his breakfast smoothie she had explained, "The color balance of the second shot was all wrong." Or, "I got the damned camera at a slight angle, it gives the tree trunk a zig-zag. I feel like such a rube, but it's good to be taking pictures again, even if it's just trees and bugs with that toy camera." Carl swallowed thoughtfully.

Billy, a student in the electronics program at College of The Redwoods made sure Carl got on all the lists for grants. That had funded the eye lid monitor. They put up a large Morse code poster on the wall opposite the hospital bed installed in Carl's bedroom. With help from the county nurse, Carl's extended family, and neighbors, Mama and Carl got by. Carl became the class project for a number of Billy's electronics and IT classmates. Three years after Carl returned from the hospital many of his former students still stopped by to assist with scrounged hardware and software for the home-brewed monitoring and communications systems that filled the shelves lining Carl's bedroom.

When Doctor Hemmings told her to leave the chemicals alone or die in a year, she'd tried digital. The digital cameras a dozen years before just weren't good enough for fashion photography. What friends she had evaporated like her career. She had allowed herself the extravagance of three full days of grief at that loss, then shopped the trade magazines for work and found a part time teaching gig at the local junior college. Nowadays she spent eighteen hours a week going through the basics of composition, structure, and how to turn the damned thing on to a bunch of people who spent too much on cameras they could never appreciate. Even when the technology improved and was accepted in the fashion magazine world she could never go back. There was no place for her in New York, and no place in her for New York any more. She could never reenter the world of glamorous, vacuous, sweaty tall people.

The accidental shot of Runt's glossy black face stared out from the monitor. Mama had to laugh. The picture was just too goofy to delete. "Well, I have to admit it is better than the mushroom."

"Okay, baby, now show us some pink!" she said to the monitor. Before haute couture, Mama had put herself through college taking pictures for "Gentleman's Magazines." Now however, the "pink" she referred to was Runt's tongue hanging out in a monstrous and elegant curve across the screen. Looking at the image with a critical eye she said to no one in particular, "Dodge out some highlights here and burn in a little detail there." She worked into the night, chatting to herself, until she said aloud, "Now that's entertainment," and laughed.

"Carl, you want to see a picture?" Carl blinked rapidly. Any diversion from non-stop sitcoms on his big screen TV was welcome. She watched as letters appeared on the small monitor on the far side of the bed spelling, "PLZ". This was their own language; a mixture of English, Morse code, and cell phone texting (which the two of them called "twit speak") mixed in with some of the vowellessness of old Hebrew. He did occasionally use vowels for clarity.

Setting her laptop on the blanket covering his motionless legs she hit a button and instantly said "Damn!" What appeared was her most recent attempt at a picture of the lone redwood stitched together. As she worked to bring up the dog picture he blinked furiously, "STP STP STP." A glance up at his monitor showed her his plea.

"You want to see the redwood?"

All he could do was blink, "YZ"

"Okay, it's not very good yet. I'm still learning how to get the frames to meld into something better than a patchwork quilt."

She saw his eyes were moist. Dabbing at the corners she asked, "You like?"

"YZ BTY"

"Beauty?"

"YZ"

"You want me to show you some others from my walk yesterday?"

"PLZ"

"Well, there's this one of that white hanging flower bush thingie."

"NDN PLM"

It took a bit of negotiation to get that he meant "Indian plum."

"You know the wildflowers?"

"YZ TRZ 2" "Trees too..."

For the rest of the evening she sat next to him on the inclined bed chatting in their way about pictures she'd taken with her little camera. When she finally did get around to the carefully edited picture of Runt he waxed eloquent by adding two vowels. "LMAO"

"Laugh My Ass Off?" She translated. "I'm glad you like it."

"CNTST"

Once again it took a minute to ascertain that he was suggesting she enter it in a contest somewhere.

"I hadn't thought of that. I mean it's goofy as all hell. I'll have to buy a magazine to see what's out there."

Two days later as she fed him breakfast while sitting on the edge of his bed she read, "WNT SLL TR3"

"Oh, Carl, you can't sell that. I mean after you put so much into it."

"CRL N DRV"

"Yeah, I know you can't drive, but would you like me to take you for a ride?"

"N CRL P N STS"

Much of their shared language was based on context and Mama's intuition. "No, Carl pee on seats." She saw from the press of his lips he was determined.

With a sigh she said, "I'll get Billy to put it online. As good as the Triumph is I'm sure you'll have no trouble selling it." They both did their best to smile.

"Oh, yeah, I entered that silly Runt picture in a magazine contest." In her best quavering evangelist voice she theatrically shook her outstretched hands and belted out, "Oh how the mighty have fallen!" She grinned ruefully. "Might as well try."

"GD LCK"

They sat on his bed and listened to the distinctive gear whine of the old sports car as it drove away. "Well, that's that." She counted the crisp one-hundred dollar bills onto his chest. "So, what do you want to do with your new-found wealth?"

"BY CMRA" he blinked out rapidly.

"Buy Camera? Well, I have to ask you the same thing I ask all my classes. What kind of pictures is this camera going to take?" They both understood the irony in her words.

"NTR"

"Nature?"

"Y"

Author's note

This story started as an exercise, trying to describe a person through the impact their history has had on a garment. To me, Mama's coat traces her history. Carl's condition scares the hell out of me. Mama makes his life tolerable

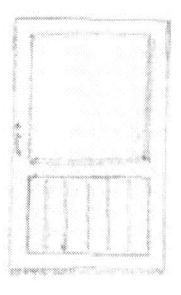

A SWIG OF COFFEE

by Shari Snowden

    In Old Town, Los Bagels is the only place open before seven for a good cup of coffee. I order a medium roasted and take my usual place by the window. The center stool has the best view of the street and the newspaper is there waiting for me. It's rumpled, a little damp. But no matter, I just pretend to read it so he don't see me watching him walk by.

    He walks straight down Second Street, never glances my way but that's okay, that's fine; I just need to see that he's alive and well for another day.

    There's a chill on the street this morning. He's wearing a cap and a warm jacket over his work shirt. His hair is turning premature gray, like mine at his age. He's clean shaven and his work boots are worn down, well used. I'd give something to know what's in his satchel. But he's legit. A working man. Just an ordinary Joe.

    I'm proud he didn't turn out like his old man: A two-bit hustling, thieving, junky-ass jailbird.

    His wife don't worry he'll be calling her for bail. She don't need to send no Dear John letter to his CDC number. And his kids, they don't worry about their pap coming home mad-drunk, dodging his fist.

    He dashes by, early today. I haven't even had time for a sip. I like to get settled in first, swirl the cream and sugar in my cup to sweeten my outlook.

    I go to the counter for a Huckleberry Danish, something extra sweet, to make up for my loss.

    To my right, a man walks into the café. It's him. He's off his routine. He's never come inside before. Good God, he steps up right next to me, orders a 16 ounce dark organic, straight up, and a scone, maple frosted.

    He feels me staring, looks my way. I'm mesmerized, can't take my eyes from his face. He has my father's eyes. My eyes.

    I drag myself back to my table with my Danish, watching him on the sly.

    He nibbles the corner of his scone.

    I munch my Danish but I'm so flustered I can't enjoy the taste.

I take a swig.

He takes a cautious sip of his steaming brew, looks my way, gives me a half-smile then snaps the lid on his cup and hurries out the door.

A remarkable likeness. Surely, he saw himself when he looked at me. No. On second thought, *hell* no. Not a trace of likeness to this old face, jowled and creviced by sixty odd years, ravaged by way of the street, by a thousand failures, by more than a decade in the slammer. All he saw was a scarred-up old derelict polluting the air at Los Bagels.

I hope somebody told him I died in the war. A gallant death. So he can be proud of his old man. So he thinks he missed out on something worthwhile. Not for my sake. I'm long past redemption, long past reform. I ain't looking for no joyful reunion. I ain't worth a plug nickel to him in this world.

I come here each morning just to see he's made it through another day. Just to see that he's walkin' the sunny side of the street. Maybe tomorrow he'll come by early and stop for a coffee. We'll have a swig together before he rushes off to work. He's the only thing on this crazy, screwed-up planet that matters to me. The only thing I care about. He's all I got.

Author's Note

It was a challenge from the Rain All Day Writers: write a complete story in 600 words or less. I was in Old Town when the story popped into my head. I saw a lonely old man with a cup of coffee watching the world go by.

This story is not like my usual stuff. It has no dialogue and it is written from the point of view of a *man*.

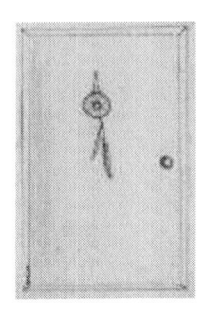

A YEAR TO FORGET

by June Nessler

"It's the kind of place where Joe is."

"Joe? Joe Who?"

"Joe Anybody. You know. When someone says, 'Whatever happened to Joe or Bob or Whoever?' You can bet he's in a little town in the boonies of Northern CA."

"Oh." Helen dug into her limp salad, the kind sometimes served in college cafeterias.

"I love it here, you know," Della said, gazing at the distant ocean through the cafeteria window next to their table. "When I first traced route 299 west from Redding on the map and realized that printed right over the city of Arcata was Humboldt State College, I knew somehow that I'd end up here. It still feels like paradise, even though I've been here for almost five years."

"Mmm." Helen's mouth was full of lettuce but she spoke over it. "How dud the rehearshal go lasht night."

Della reddened. "It was the most embarrassing episode I've had in the last ten or twenty years."

"Mmm?"

"I've sung with orchestras, you know, dance bands and stuff. But singing with the Humboldt State Symphony Orchestra was really different. I'm telling you, I wanted to die. I made at least four false starts. Vivaldi was turning over in his grave! I finally got it right; but the after-burn of embarrassment is still with me. It's no wonder a lot of instrumentalists don't think much of singers."

"It probably wasn't that bad," Helen commiserated.

"You had to be there."

A group of students entered the college cafeteria raising a din that precluded further conversation. When the noise died down, Della grimaced and said, "Now that I think about it objectively, I mean about that town, the one where Joe is, I really think a concerted effort to oust us had been in play for months, and I wonder that I was never aware of it." She paused a beat, shook her head slowly and said, "We should have listened."

"Listened to what?"

"Well, to begin with, Dr. Dolph Nyhoffer, short for Adolph, the town's only doctor, needed help caring for his patients. So he hired Dr. Jeffrey Banks. Banks was leaving, and Ben was taking his place. The day after we arrived, Banks visited us ostensibly to welcome us as well as to say good-bye. We talk a while and eventually he said, 'I wouldn't feel right if I didn't warn you about this place and Dolph Nyhoffer.'"

"Warn you?" queried Helen.

"Yes, and warn us he did. He said that whenever things went wrong, say with a patient or if some medical error was made, Ben, even though blameless, would have the finger pointed at him by Dr. Adolph Nyhoffer. And then he emphasized that Nyhoffer and his wife Winona were a power in the community. Above all, they controlled the rumor mill."

Helen said, "Let me guess. You didn't believe a word of what Banks told you."

Della nodded. "We took him for a disgruntled person who was holding a grudge for some reason."

They were silent for a moment as they ate their lunch. Then Helen said hesitantly, "Look, I have an assignment where I have to interview someone. How would you like to be my interviewee?"

"Oh sure. Everyone at this college wants to hear my stored-up gems of wisdom."

"It's for a journalism course. It would help me a lot. We could start with how you got to Humboldt County."

Della said, "Well, OK, we travelled south from Philly and hooked up with route 66 in Missouri. Somehow we managed to reach interstate 5 in California, lost our way for a few miles when we tried for the coast. We made it to Joe's town in time for Ben to take over the spot vacated by Jeffrey Banks. That's how we got here."

"No, no, Wiseass, I mean, what motivated you?" Helen retrieved a large yellow pad and pen from her backpack. "Start from the time you got to Humboldt County. It's got to be a strange story, your traveling across the country and ending up in a strange little town in Far Northern California."

"Not so strange," replied Della. "Ben finished his medical internship in Philadelphia, and we wanted to go to the West Coast. There were a lot of places we could have gone because doctors are a scarce commodity in a lot of rural areas."

"But why that particular town?"

"Hah! We researched different rural places, looking mostly for good weather. The town seemed to have just the right climate. No snow, no fog, lots of greenery, and especially, no rain in the summer…and…it's in

California... a big plus. Everyone I knew in Philly wanted to come to California. Those that had made the trip couldn't stop talking about how great it was out here."

Helen wrote as Della spoke and stopped when she stopped. Della leaned toward her friend and said, "Am I talking too fast?"

"Shorthand. I'm good at it," was Helen's reply. Then she said, "You being from a big city must have been a little surprised when you saw the place where you had chosen to live."

"I don't think surprised is the word for what I felt when I struggled out of my sleeping bag--we had no furniture--that first morning and peeked through the drapes. I don't know what I expected to see, but it was not a herd? A gaggle? A squad? A pod? What's a bunch of pigs called?"

"Haven't the slightest," said Helen.

"Anyhow they were heading over the field toward our house. Nine. There were nine of them! They eventually made themselves comfortable by lying down on the narrow cement walkway that separated our house from the bare, clay-colored front yard."

"I'm trying to picture your expression at the sight," laughed Helen.

"I was speechless. Our two kids were still asleep when Ben got up. He was as boggled as I was when he saw the pigs blocking the front door. He said he was going to do something about it. Like complain or something."

"What did you do?"

"Used the back door."

"No," Helen laughed, "I mean about the pigs."

"Nothing. There was nothing to do but to get along with not only pigs but other critters who roamed the open range. That's what it was called. Open range. It means that animals, instead of being fenced in, are allowed to roam wherever they please. Well, at least the kids learned to identify non-cartoon barnyard animals. They wouldn't have learned that in Philadelphia." Della wrinkled her nose. "Every so often I had to muck out what I laughingly called the front yard so the kids wouldn't step in any crap." She shrugged, "I became used to it." She took a large bite of her sandwich and chewed.

Helen waited and then asked, "Were the people friendly?"

"At first I thought they really were good, generous people," replied Della.

"What do you mean by 'at first?'" asked Helen, looking up from her scribbling.

Della continued. "Shortly after we arrived, a man brought us a fresh salmon that he'd caught from the Trinity River. It was huge! I had no idea what we'd do with so much salmon. But his wife took me to her house and taught me how to preserve it in small jars. The jars kept us in salmon for a year." She paused, thinking. "I was not really without friends, in the beginning."

"Do I hear a reservation in that mild declaration?"

"I had friends but there was no one I could really talk to. If I complained about anything, in a flash it was all over the town. You know what I mean? Once I remarked to a visitor that there was a stray dog that would bully Schultz, our German shepherd puppy. Next morning, first thing, I looked out the living room window. A guy was aiming a rifle at the stray that usually slept on the walkway in front of our house! To my utter shock and horror, he shot the poor animal right there, outside our door! But he only wounded it, and the dog ran away howling pitifully. It must have died somewhere. Oh god! I still think of that poor animal and the pain and shock that it must have felt."

Helen said, "That was some experience!"

"I'm still carrying the guilt about what happened to that dog," said Della. Tears threatened but she swiped at them, warding them off. "That was one of the first things in the accumulation of the reasons the town had for not liking me ... us... very much."

"What?" Helen stared at her friend. "What do you mean?"

"Well, the worst thing is that most of the people in the town felt I was to blame for that dog, not the guy who shot it."

"Strange how things like that work out," said Helen. The yellow pad was half-full with her scratchings.

"We lived within walking distance of the Trinity River. One of the first things I noticed, as Ben, the kids and I first entered Northern California was the color of the rivers and streams. Aquamarine! The only rivers I knew near Philadelphia were grey and yucky-looking. I swear they'd ignite if a lighted match were thrown into any one of them! And as for swimming, you'd have to be crazy to even think about it. But here, very near to our house, was this clear-flowing, emerald-green, tree-lined Trinity River. The kids and I spent a lot of time swimming in it." Della paused, thinking for a beat. "But it wasn't just the fun of swimming. I went there to avoid visitors."

"Visitors?"

"Visitors," said Della. "It was the major form of entertainment in the town. There were no movies, no television reception, and little radio reception. I soon realized that I was to have visitors all day long while they waited their turn to see their doctor. The office was less than a tenth of a mile away from our house."

"You mean that people you hardly knew or didn't know would just drop in?" asked Helen.

"Oh yes," said Della. "And not one of them seemed to think they were inconveniencing me. I served coffee and something to go with it. I didn't say much to them outside of mundane remarks about the weather...stuff like that. The dog incident taught me that any inadvertent slip of the tongue by the new doctor's wife got repeated and, worse, acted on within hours."

"That's awful," said Helen. "How did you cope?"

"Escaped to the river with the kids as soon as Ben left the house in the morning, around 7:30." Della took another slug of coke. "But there is something that sticks in my mind about being at the river. And now that I am thinking about it, it's beginning to make sense." She began to nod as though agreeing with an idea that had just come to her. "Other mothers used to come to the river with their kids. They were friendly enough. We talked about kids and cooking and other commonplace things." Della stopped, as though she had come to a realization. "I guess I didn't notice any coolness that sprang up between them and me at first. I used to read a lot when I was on that beach. One day some of their conversation penetrated through my reading. I heard Jew mentioned." Della turned to Helen. "Ben's Jewish, you know."

"Well?" said Helen.

"Well, my ears perked up for that reason. I listened as these women used the usual disparaging clichés. I was confused. When had they ever met any Jewish people? There were no Jews in the town. Probably never had been before Ben. The only place they could have learned anything about Jews was at church." Della turned to Helen. "I would never allow my kids into a church. 'If you want to raise bigots, send 'em to church,' I always say."

"I don't agree," Helen said.

"Oh well, that's neither here nor there. But, now I realize that the conversation among these women was for my benefit. Dolph Nyhoffer and his wife knew that Ben was Jewish, I'm sure. Did I tell you that Winona Nyhoffer was a member of the local Indian tribe?"

"No. But that's interesting. That would make them a power in a community with a high Native American population."

Helen sighed, "Those little 'beach conversations' started about the time the trouble between Ben and his boss was coming to a head."

"You mean to say that the conversations were deliberately staged to alienate you?"

"I really can't think otherwise. But I didn't figure it out at the time. I guess my problems started when people blamed me for the dog incident.. Then, when I was no longer available to serve coffee and donuts to the waiting-room crowd, it was another reason to resent me." Della paused before summing up. "Well, you know me...big mouth. I made one gaff after another that reinforced the effort to have Ben and me leave the community. The worst thing that happened was when we had no running water."

"Was there a drought?" Helen asked.

"No, nothing like that," said Della. "The owner of our house had some differences with the family that was supplying our water, so the family turned it off."

"Just like that?"

"Yep. No warning; one morning there was no water." Della smiled. "I wondered what my friends in Philadelphia would have thought if they had seen me and the kids bathing ourselves in the Trinity River, or collecting drinking water from a spring miles away. I used to fill every empty container I had, but there was never enough water for everything...you know, toilets and stuff. It was that way all summer. We left in September."

Helen shook her head smiling ruefully.

"The thing was that the family who turned off the water also owned the house where Nyhoffer and Ben had their office."

"Whoa!" Said Helen. "You mean that the good Dr. Nyhoffer might have had the power to turn the situation around, and he didn't do it?"

"He didn't make any effort to do so even though his wife commiserated with me about the inconvenience it caused our family. That part was a sham, of course." Della took a sip of coke. "I was friends with the nurses at the small hospital. It was located just outside our back yard. Well, one of the nurses hooked up a hose to a faucet outside the hospital and ran it up to our backdoor so that we'd have access to water. She would have been fired if there hadn't been a shortage of hospital staff. When the administrator found out about it, there was a hullabaloo, and the hose was disconnected. I thought the powers that be at the hospital would want to help us. After all, Ben had patients there and he himself was there a lot of the time."

"Sounds like you really were on your own," said Helen.

"We were. Ben was becoming more and more morose and very hard to live with. He must have really pissed off his boss. Probably the other way around, too. I didn't want to live that way. One day I explained to Ben that, even though we had bought a beautiful property above the town, I wanted to leave. I said we didn't belong there, and besides, we weren't wanted. I was adamant. I think he was relieved to tell everyone that he was leaving because his wife was unhappy and wanted to leave."

"And so you left."

"Let's face it, Helen, we were run out of town." Della laughed quietly. "Of all the things that I thought might happen to me in my lifetime, being run out of town was not one of them."

"Hey listen," said Helen, "It was a unique experience."

"Yes it was," replied Della. She raised her coke can. "Bless them all, the Nyhoffers and their entourage of fawning townspeople! I'd still be living there, feeling as low as a snake's belly in a wagon rut, if everything had gone right for Ben and me." After she gulped down the coke toast, she said, " OK, enough of the *stürm und drang*, the misery! It's no longer a part of my life. Let's get out of here." She looked at her watch. "Keep your fingers crossed because I have another Vivaldi rehearsal in ten minutes."

As the women were about to leave, Della put her hand on Helen's arm and said, "Thanks for persuading me to tell that story."

"Why?" asked Helen. "You were doing me a big favor. My assignment for the week is complete. I should be thanking you."

Della said, "I've always carried a negative, resentful feeling for that year. But after telling you the story, the whole year has become a tiresome episode that is best forgotten."

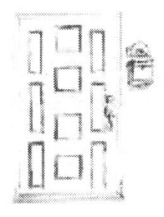

A WIDE SPOT IN THE ROAD

by Anthony Westkamper

The long days of summer gave Jack the opportunity he needed after work to take his motorcycle for an evening ride east up Highway 36. A late start restricted this particular excursion to the big turn-around at the west end of the bridge that gives Bridgeville its name. It was only a ten mile trip, but the beautiful scenery and challenging road made it worth getting suited up.

Picking a good line through the twisties, getting the lean just right, and rolling on the throttle as he passed through the apex of each turn was about as close to Zen as he could manage. Tonight he was in a good groove, doing a couple of lazy loops when he reached the turnout.

Kickstand down, ignition key off, gloves off, helmet visor up, glasses off, helmet off, ignition key lanyard over left wrist, ear plugs out and into jeans watch pocket. It was so routine he hardly noticed. This night he looked forward to sitting on the low fence rail, sipping at the hot coffee from his thermos, and just being. Sometimes cars went by, on another occasion several weeks earlier another motorcyclist had stopped on a rat Harley and they talked, but usually it was quiet. Thinking was an option he was not planning on exercising this evening.

Not expecting any interruption he allowed the patterns of steam in the thermos top cup to absorb his attention.

"You going to Eureka? Can I get a little help?" It took a while for the words to penetrate his reverie. Later, he would realize that he'd been hearing them for a little while. Looking around he saw no one, imagined that he'd imagined the tiny sounds, and went back to meditating on the shifting mist coming from the coffee.

"Can I get a little help?" Now he was sure he was actually hearing a person, not some audible mirage or words from a distant radio. Feeling put upon he dragged his thoughts out of the coffee cup, and stood, peering into the underbrush along the sides of the road. On the other side of the road sat a tiny figure among the weeds. The frail voice plaintively asked, "You going to Eureka?"

"No." He said firmly.

"Too bad. Can I get a little help?"

A car passed between the two going west. "Thanks a lot." The tiny voice carried. Jack was bemused to see a middle finger extended at the receding tail lights.

Without bothering to look both ways he crossed the road and stood in front of a tiny brown woman sitting on the asphalt berm with her feet on the road.

"Can I get a little help?"

"What kind of help?" Leery of strangers, especially ones in unexpected circumstances Jack watched carefully for signs of danger.

"Nice bike," she said looking up at him with a can of Natural Ice something in one hand and a home rolled cigarette in the other.

"Thanks," he said, thinking to himself, I don't like drunks!

"Sure you're not going to Eureka? I was looking to camp down there behind the Mall." The alcohol seemed to dissolve the hard edges off her consonants. She had a tiny round lined walnut of a face and longish black hair streaked with gray, parted in the middle and pulled straight back. Just below her mouth were what looked like two raised downward pointing brown triangular moles. He guessed she was a local Native American. She wore a drab t-shirt under a button up t-shirt under a heavier olive outer shirt.

"No, I'm not going to Eureka tonight. Besides you don't have a helmet and if I get caught giving you a ride we both get a two-hundred-and-fifty dollar fine." Explaining himself felt weak, but it was the truth.

"Too bad. I was looking to camp down behind the Mall."

"Yeah, I got that." An olive colored sleeping bag was wrapped over her legs. Despite several hand sewn patches it was leaking white synthetic filler from more than one place. There was a new-looking backpack in the weeds beside her.

"Well, can you help me over to the other side of the road? Doesn't look like I'll get picked up over here." She gathered up her sleeping bag, and offered it to him. Leaning over he picked up the backpack too. There was something in the sleeping bag, but he wasn't curious at all. A horn handle stuck out of the backpack. He guessed it might be attached to a large knife.

Setting the bundle and knapsack down next to the rail where he'd been sitting, he trudged back across the road to her. She was scratching at large patches of skin on the backs of her hands. They looked like psoriasis plaques. Leaning back she plucked a vibrant purple vetch blossom. As she daintily trimmed off excess leaves and vine he noted the lengthening shadows. She handed him the flower.

"Thanks," he said, pinning its stem under the strap on his jacket collar. She rocked back and tried to stand up. That didn't work so he offered her his hand. She snubbed out the cigarette on the ground and with a bit of help managed to get to her feet. The top of her head was almost level with his shoulder. Jack, being about five feet nine, guessed she was a bit less than five feet tall.

"I'm gonna need some help. You might have to carry me across." Even close up her voice was tiny and plaintive.

Despite the fact that she might weigh ninety pounds including her can of malt, there was no way Jack wanted to get that intimate.

"Can't do that. I blew out my hip a while back and can't carry much now," he said, reminding himself that the accident hadn't prevented him from righting the six hundred pound bike when he'd dropped it.

"I got hit by a car and they're supposed to put a pin in my hip." Resting her hand on his forearm to steady herself, she bent over, sat the can on the raised berm, and hiked up her pant leg, displaying an Ace bandage.

Struggling to keep the insincerity he felt out of his voice he said, "Wow!"

Retrieving her drink she stood and they proceeded across the road. The burden of her hand on his forearm had all the weight of a parakeet. Looking down on the scene in his mind's eye he was amused by how solemn and formal it must have looked. It was like a scene from an old movie. He was the gent escorting a lady across a road as she carries her cocktail. He wondered if the heavy road rash resistant motorcycle jacket was also cootie proof, and felt annoyed at feeling guilty for having such thoughts.

Getting her settled on the fence next to her knapsack and the old sleeping bag she looked up at him and said, "I gotta' piss something awful." Jack rolled his eyes, said nothing, and made his way back towards the bike. Stowing the thermos in the panniers he pulled out a moist antibacterial towelette, scrubbed his hands and the arm of his jacket. A bit of worry crept into him, wondering if she knew enough to protect herself from the damp cold creeping up from the river below.

"I got family back in the woods." Her frail voice seemed no louder, but carried in the quiet.

"Can I call someone for you when I get home?"

"Nah, they ain't got a phone."

Reaching once again into his luggage Jack pulled out a nutrition bar guaranteed to have just the right ratios of protein, carbohydrates, and fats as specified by the most recent diet fad. The label said "Raspberry Chocolate." Hell, he thought, maybe it'll help her.

Returning to her one more time he handed her the package. "Here, this has lots of nutrition and stuff in it. They're a bit dry, but I like 'em well enough."

"Oh, thank you. You're nice."

He smiled, made a slight bow turning once again toward the bike. "Thanks. Good luck. Hope you get a ride."

Ear plugs in, helmet on, glasses on, gloves on. Despite the expanding foam filling his ear canals he heard her say, "Ooh, raspberry. This is good. Makes me feel kinda' horny."

Kickstand up, key in ignition, kick transmission to neutral, press starter button, bip throttle, and he was away. Kick up to second gear, wave goodbye without looking back and focus attention on the twisties, looking out for deer and skunks. "Damn!" he said to the inside of his helmet.

Mick and the fellows were working their way through *Street Fighting Man* as Jack, back from his ride, shredded cheddar into the saucepan of hot milk. Adding cayenne pepper, a touch of flour, and crumbled bacon, he hummed as he worked. Dropping the knob on the toaster as the Stones slipped into *Jumpin' Jack Flash*. Once the cheese melted he stopped to pour in half a cup of beer and stirred rapidly, eyeing it for a smooth consistency as it came back up to temperature.

"Timing is everything!" He exclaimed to Ajax the cockatiel, as he poured the cheese sauce over a toasted English muffin.

Holding up a forkful of dripping Welsh Rarebit he said, "Better than a raspberry chocolate protein bar! I tell you, Ajax, there was something weird about that little old lady," and chuckled. Routines helped fill the place in his life that Suzanne left when she passed away.

Later when the pots and dishes were nestled in the drying rack he changed the water in the bird cage saying, "Looks like it'll be a Green Fairy night tonight." Ajax was non-committal.

The routine of dribbling water through a sugar cube into the emerald absinthe was another way to fill the hollow hours while he waited for sleep to finally give him rest.

"Can I get some help?"

Jack seldom remembered his dreams, and those he remembered were never so obviously connected to the waking world. She was sitting on the rail where he'd left her. Smoke from a fresh rolled cigarette drifted straight up before it broke into a knot of turbulence.

Jack looked around. He was in his cooking apron and underpants.

Vulnerable....Looking around he made a surprised face; nudity or partial nudity in dreams indicated a feeling of vulnerability. As soon as he thought that it might be cold it certainly was. Damn, he thought. I wish I hadn't thought of that! Behind him his bike was up on the center stand with his riding clothes draped across the saddle.

"Wait a minute," he said donning the pants, undershirt and jacket. On the ground on the far side of the bike were his heavy riding boots and socks.

"Take your time!" The voice sounded sure and firm. "I've got all the time in the world!" She laughed.

"So, what's up?" Jack found it easy to fit into this dream now that he was clothed and warm.

"I don't know. I mean you called me." The little face split into a wide grin. "Maybe you need a little help."

"You sound different. More..." His voice trailed off as he tried to come up with the word.

"More here?" Once again she was smiling. "That's because my time in your world was running out. I was kind of fading. Then again it might have been that malt liquor I was drinking. Can't get that where I come from. Prohibition was never repealed." Jack reminded himself even in a dream he shouldn't stand there with his mouth open looking stupid.

Suddenly, they were sitting on the fence rail, side by side, bent over, resting elbows on knees.

"Different worlds have different rules. In yours everybody dies, no choice about it. Where I come from everyone is born immortal though most folks eventually opt out after a few hundred years. I'm one of the fighters. I want to live forever." She toasted him with a can.

Going along with the dream Jack said. "So, why are we here? What's up?"

"You called me!" Somehow the woman seemed more real than she had in the flesh.

"Called? I got drunk and went to sleep. How'd I call you?"

"Welsh Rarebit and absinthe, whoo! That mix was sure to give you dreams." She smiled mischievously.

"So, you're the stuff of dreams?" A host of implications flooded his mind. Not the least of which was his impending insanity.

"No, I'm real enough, the dreamscape is just a convenient place to meet. It's easier than actually manifesting in your world. I shouldn't keep that up for very long."

"Then why do it at all? I mean what were you doing in my world?"

"First, I was in your world up there on the road enjoying myself. Along with immortality there are other big differences in our worlds. For one, no booze! Another is lots of people. Every square inch is under cultivation, covered with homes, or under some sort of control. There are ever so many laws and rules there. Some of us come to Earth to get away from that. You folks at least still have a few wild places where an unexpected animal might pop out and surprise you. I like the randomness. So, when it gets to be too much I make the trip." Her words were clear and sharp now. "Over the years fewer and fewer of us do. It seems to be getting harder. They say the dimensions are getting farther apart or something."

"So why are we talking in a dream?" Jack looked at his hands.

Her tiny wrinkled face scrunched up in concentration. She said, "Actually I don't remember much about my last visit, the one where we met... I'm really unaccustomed to alcohol." She looked embarrassed at the admission. "But I do remember you seemed nice but profoundly sad. I felt a pull and thought maybe I could help. When you fell asleep, I used some of the old craft and here we are!" A happy wide smile brightened her face.

John looked down at his hands and pressed his lips together. "I'm not sad. Not really. Sometimes I get a bit lonely, since Suzanne passed. You know... died. But I've got Ajax, and there's the place to take care of, and..." He looked down again.

"Before you ask, no, there isn't a Suzanne in my world, and I may be a forest elf or leprechaun or fairy but I can't bring back the dead. My world or this one, dead is dead. Sorry."

"Yeah, I figured. So, how often do you make it to Earth anyway?" He asked softly.

"How often do you ride that murdercycle up to the wide spot?"

"Oh, whenever the house gets too big and quiet for me. How about you?" He asked, looking straight ahead.

"I go there when my place gets too claustrophobic and noisy." She chuckled softly. "This last time, I got carried away, stayed too long and lost focus. I let myself go. I had that nasty skin condition and arthritis in my hip. It'll be a while before I can comfortably manifest in your world again."

They both stared at a gum spot on the pavement a few feet away.

Quietly she said, "After that, if you dream about me again, I'll hear you. You could bring a can of beer and we can meet up there again if you'd like. Maybe next time you could bring a helmet."

Author's Note

I ride my motorcycle up to the wide spot next to the bridge at Bridgeville. It is isolated and alone and a good place to meditate whilst sipping coffee and wondering how magical critters work. I wonder what their physics, history, and philosophy books say. While this little lady hints at some of it, much still remains a mystery to Jack.

DEEP DOWN THINGS

by Lisa Baney

Before the world was we lived as one in the light and song of eternity. There was no time, no unhappiness.
This lasted forever.

Rae muttered, "Come on, come on," and bobbed her head up and down to peer around the bodies massed on the Plaza. She looked at her watch—still 10:08—and then sneaked a quick glance at the Farmer's Market program manager, just in time to catch the frown he threw her.

Ann Marie said, "Why don't we start without her?"

Rae gave her a look. "Right. You sing soprano." Ann Marie was the tenor, her voice deep and rich and smoky, which regularly incited in Rae a secret envy.

Ann Marie let out a *pffft* of a laugh. "Ha ha. We *could* do an ensemble number. The new one, maybe. Or the improv."

Rae looked again into the crowd, willing Cherrie to show her pouty face. She had thought to hold the ensemble pieces as emergency backups in case they ran short or—and she hated the prescience in this—in case Cherrie decided not to show. But—and she looked at her watch again (10:09)—even if they started right this minute they wouldn't probably even have time for all of the contingency tunes. The next band was supposed to go on in twenty minutes.

"OK," Rae sighed. "Let's just start. Marla, let's go with the improv."

Marla was leaning against a lamppost, watching the crowd with a bored alertness, her long legs stretched out in front of her. She pushed herself upright. "What a bitch," she said. "Whaddaya wanna bet she's still in bed shagging some guy—"

"Marla, shh!" Rae flashed another look at the program manager. He had his back to them, but singers had to be careful. Their voices carried a lot further than regular people's. If these amateurs—Ann Marie and Marla and

Cherrie—ever had to make a living in the music business they'd know that. Oh-ho, would they ever.

Rae turned and caught Marla and Ann Marie looking at each other and rolling their eyes. Yes, all right, fine, she was a nag. But what did they know really?

When they were in place on the small stage Rae stepped up to her mic and took a breath. "Hi everyone," she said to the crowd, which was largely unaware of them, huddled in fleeces and wool jackets against the cold overcast November morning. "Welcome to the last Arcata Farmer's Market of the year! We're the Divas and we'll be singing a few tunes for you this morning."

Rae raised the icy pitch-pipe to her lips, blew a note, and Marla started them off with a tempo, a groove and a simple four-bar line, one they'd come up with in rehearsal. Ann Marie and Rae started snapping their fingers, and then there was no room to think about anything other than what was happening with the music. It went surprisingly well with just the three of them, Rae thought.

Anyway it could've gone much, much worse.

As she was introducing the next tune Rae felt a tug on the back of her jacket. In mid-sentence she turned to look behind her. There was Cherrie, in oversized sunglasses despite the day's gloom, black jacket buttoned up one button off, her hair smashed flat on one side and teased to bouffant ridiculousness on the other. Even from a distance she reeked of un-metabolized alcohol and recent sex.

"Hiiiiii," she sang out. "I'm heeeeerrrre!"

"What are you doing?" Rae managed through clenched teeth. "Get up on the stand."

Cherrie jiggled on one leg and stretched her messily lipsticked mouth into a long line. "I have to peeeeee," she said in a little-girl voice. "Pweez Mommy, can I go to da bafwoom?"

Incredulous, Rae stared at her. "What? No! No, you can't go to the bathroom." Rae was having trouble holding her voice down. "Get your ass up here. Right now! We only have another couple of songs."

Afterwards, thinking about the events of the next ten minutes, Rae decided she couldn't come up with a more humiliating moment over her entire performing career. If she didn't know better she would've thought Cherrie's performance was a deliberate burlesque, complete with pratfall, furious stage-whispered skirmish with Marla, several off-key entrances, and finally, as if rehearsed to perfection, a long belch squarely on mic. A crowd of young guys stopped to watch them, laughing and clapping at each one of Cherrie's antics.

Great, Rae said to herself, thinking of all the time they'd spent rehearsing for today. So glad we're getting all this great exposure. This is sure to get us more gigs.

The program manager came over and handed Rae their pay, a cell phone clamped to his ear, and walked away without talking to them. Rae suspected gloomily that he was faking a call. She gave Marla and Ann Marie their cuts in silence.

"Thanks," murmured Anne Marie, her forehead wrinkled in concern as she looked up into Rae's face and patted her arm. "I think we sounded really great." That was Ann Marie, ever the consoling mom. Rae smiled thinly.

Marla took her pay and stalked away without saying a word.

Cherrie was talking and posturing with the group of guys; Rae stood watching for a moment before calling out, "Cherrie. Here." She lifted her hand with Cherrie's take and then put the money on the ground, anchoring it with her half-empty water bottle.

"Bye Mom!" Cherrie called out, and the guys laughed again. One of them said, "Is she the boss?" and Cherrie answered, "Man, *is* she!" Then, predictably, more laughter.

As she made her way across the Plaza, her battered gig bag bumping the back of her knee with every other step, a spry woman in baggy jeans and beach-worthy hat strode up to her and held out her hand.

"Thank you so much for your lovely music," she quavered. "I haven't heard 'Mr. Sandman' done so well since I saw the Chordettes in concert many years ago. You sounded just like them!"

Rae gaped at the woman and took her hand without thinking. "Thank you," she said automatically. "We had a lot of fun," which was her standard reply to musical praise no matter how bad the performance. Then she added, surprising herself with the emotion in her words, "We worked really hard on that song. It's really difficult singing those sixth chords in such close harmony without accompaniment."

"Yes, indeed," agreed the woman. Her eyes were amazing, Rae thought. So large and dark and expressive.

"We spent a lot of time rehearsing," Rae went on, realizing she was talking too much and feeling sudden, incongruous tears prickling her eyelids.

The woman smiled at her. She really did have incredible eyes, almost like reflective pools. "Oh, I believe it. You can't just open your mouth and have wonderful music come out without being ready for it."

Rae blinked at the woman. "Thank you," she said, and then, again, "Thank you."

Eventually, after many eternities, a time came when we were to leave the place of our beginning, and a great and eternal glass was fashioned of the light and music and color and beauty of all things. When we gazed into the glass we saw within its depths ourselves as we truly were, made of the intricate fabric of forever, all the same, all created to be joy.

It was raining so hard the night of the yearly party for the Humboldt County Artists' Collective it felt like a resentful caddy was hurling golf balls from above and deliberately aiming for heads. Rae got to the Morris Graves Museum early and made sure the PA was set up for them—they were opening the entertainment part of the evening—and then went downstairs to change and fix her hair. Ann Marie was just coming in the door, shaking out her umbrella and stamping the rain from her feet, as Rae came upstairs.

"I'm glad you're early," Rae said. "I was thinking maybe you and I could go over the middle of the do-wop medley before everyone else got here."

"Sure," Ann Marie murmured tonelessly.

Rae peered at her. "You OK?"

Ann Marie looked down, unbuttoning her raincoat with meticulous attention. "Mm-hmm." She shrugged out of the coat.

"Wow," said Rae. "That's some little black dress." She'd never seen the usually modest Ann Marie so uncovered before. She looked beautiful and provocative—and very un-Ann Marie. "I didn't even know you owned anything like that."

Ann Marie gave her a fleeting half-smile. "Yeah, well."

There was a puzzling silence.

Into it Rae said, "I think we can do this downstairs in the office;" and then saw Marla and Cherrie through the beveled glass of the entryway, racing up the stone steps so close to each other their umbrellas were clashing together as if they, too, were bickering.

"Ah, *jeez*," Rae said under her breath. Just once, couldn't those two get along? She glanced at her watch. At least everyone was here early enough to warm up and go over some sticky parts of a couple of tunes. Tonight they had to be absolutely perfect.

As Cherrie and Marla took off their wet things Rae maneuvered herself next to Marla. "Thanks for picking Cherrie up," she said softly. "I know how it must have annoyed. It really helps out the entire group, though."

Marla gave her a lopsided smile. "Anything for the group," she said. "I guess." She, too, looked beautiful tonight, in a shimmery black sheath and rhinestone earrings. In fact, they all looked great, even Cherrie, who had toned down her usual slutty look. Her makeup was subtle, her skirt just above the knee and the bodice, if not exactly high-necked, at least not threatening to suddenly rip apart and spill all. The small place in Rae's chest that had been clenched hard for a week began to relax a bit. They were going to be great tonight. Finally, a fun, professional gig. She felt light-hearted with anticipation.

After their warm-up, as they were headed upstairs, Rae reached out and touched Cherrie's arm; the other two went on. "Hey," Rae said.

Cherrie looked around from the step above.

"Take it easy on the drinking tonight. Wait until after we're done."

Cherrie pouted down at her. "O*kay*," she said.

"I mean it, Cherrie. This is an important gig."

Cherrie looked skyward and sighed, tapping the toe of her stiletto impatiently. "All *right*. I *said* I would, didn't I?"

"Good," said Rae, unruffled. "I think we'll have fun tonight."

There was a large crowd now in the main part of the gallery, people in sleek evening dress sipping champagne from stemmy crystal and conversing in small, glittering groups. Trills of laughter silvered randomly around the room, which was warm and filled with tantalizing aromas from the lidded casseroles on the buffet table. Rae's feeling of well-being grew.

She'd lost track of the others, but they knew to keep an eye on the stage area. In the crowd she saw the director of the Collective; Rae began to make her way to her, trying to be as non-intrusive as possible moving through the close-packed gathering, murmuring "Excuse me, sorry" as she brushed against silk and cashmere, the occasional bead-incrusted evening jacket.

The director was flushed with high spirits. Dangling, rectangular earrings made of some kind of iridescent glass dragged at her ear lobes, brushing the tops of her plump shoulders when she moved. Rae stared at them as they twisted and swung and flashed with reflected light.

"We're *so* excited to *have* you here!" the woman enthused. She held a glass of red wine loosely in one manicured hand; it threatened to fling amoebas of itself onto Rae with every emphasized word. "You girls are *so* beautiful and *so* talented! I can *hardly wait* to hear what you'll be *singing* tonight!"

Rae felt the tiniest twinge of superstitious dread. No, no, she told herself, Cherrie's behaving, and you know how great she sounds when she's together. Just relax, everything's fine.

The director excused herself and began to make her way to the mic, pausing every few steps to exclaim "Hel*lo*, how *are* you?" to a guest she was nose to nose with. As she neared the stage area the crowd gradually bunched forward to form a ragged crescent around the front of the room. Time to gather up the Divas.

There was room to move now. Rae looked around and spotted Cherrie. As she approached her she surreptitiously sniffed at Cherrie's breath. No alcoholic fumes. Thank you, goddess.

Cherrie caught the sniffing and gave her trademark sigh. "I'm not drinking anything! I told you. I'm waiting until after."

"Thank you," said Rae.

The director was acknowledging people now. They had maybe five minutes. Rae swiveled around to look for Marla and Ann Marie. She saw Marla leaning against a wall in the foyer, her long legs stretched out in front of her, staring out at the rain. She called to her in a carrying whisper, motioned her over.

"But," said Cherrie.

Rae was searching the room for Ann Marie now. "Hm?"

"I didn't think Ann Marie drank."

"She doesn't." Where *was* she?

Cherrie smirked. "Oh really."

Caught by Cherrie's tone, Rae glanced at her and then followed the path of her gaze. On the far side of the gathered crowd, in front of the little bar, Ann Marie was just putting one empty champagne glass down and picking up another.

Rae's breath rushed out of her in a long, wailing "N*oooooo!*"

"That's at least her fourth," Cherrie said with evident spite.

"Ann *Marie*," Rae groaned, sudden panic tightening her chest. "What are you *doing?*"

She took off across the room as if pursued by wolves. Dimly, she was aware of the director saying, "And in a *minute* we'll be hearing from one of the county's *newest* and most *lovely* group of women you'd *ever* want to *meet!*" Rae caught up to Ann Marie just as she was lifting her glass to drain it.

"No no no *no no*." Rae snatched the champagne flute out of Ann Marie's hand. "Why are you doing this? We have to sing!"

Ann Marie's eyes were half-lidded, her smile lazy and unfocused. "Don' worry, my friend. My good, good friend. Rae. You worry too much, you know that?"

Rae grabbed Ann Marie's limp arm and shook it. "Listen to me," she rasped. "You are going to sing in front of a hundred people in two minutes. This should scare you stone sober."

Ann Marie leaned her head on Rae's shoulder. "Oh, go fuck yourself," she slurred and slid her free arm around Rae's waist. "Fuck fuck fuck. Everybody's fucking." She began to nuzzle Rae's neck.

A handful of people in the crowd were casting curious, annoyed glances at them, had been for a while, Rae realized suddenly, and, disentangling herself from Ann Marie's embrace, she dragged her back across the room to join Marla and Cherrie.

"What the hell," Marla said, staring at Ann Marie. "God damn it!"

Rae looked into Marla's outraged eyes. "We have to support her. Help me keep her upright."

"Support her? She's the *tenor*. She's supposed to support *us*." Marla closed her eyes and shook her head. "Man, this is so effing amateur. "

Rae looked around at Cherrie, silent throughout this exchange, and saw her staring fixedly at Ann Marie, her look of malice having given way to a dawning terror. But she's sober, Rae thought fleetingly, and a stab of gratitude shot through her.

She pulled Marla and Cherrie close, Ann Marie in their center. "OK," she said, her voice low and urgent. "Listen to me. We are going to get through this."

"God damn—" Marla began and Rae hissed "*Shhh.*" She gave a small shake to Cherrie's arm, forcing her to meet her eyes. "Cherrie, sing out and proud and sweet. You're our lead. Remember how awesome you are."

Cherrie's face was still slack with fear, but she nodded.

"And *now*, ladies and gentlemen," the director was saying, and over her Rae said, "Marla, stay with me. You know how. We back Cherrie and we love her up."

Marla's face creased in disbelief. "We *what?*"

"...a *big* hand for the *amazing* Divas!"

Rae said, "Marla. Go!" the room erupted into applause, and the Divas, heads high, backs straight, legs flashing, strutted up onto the stage in all their sass and gorgeousness and proceeded to blow everyone away with their awesome voices.

That's how Rae wished she could remember the evening.

Then was the earth made, with its darkness and tears and sighs, and we took form there to learn the ways of that place.

The bar was almost empty early Tuesday night. Ann Marie came through the door in a rush, a fine netting of rain following her in and settling on the rough floor like a discarded overskirt of fine tulle.

"Hi," Rae called from her table. Ann Marie turned, face tense and set, flushed from the cold. Her eyes, bare of the usual makeup, looked small and stark in her pale face—the legacy of natural blondes, Rae thought.

"You look like you just dragged yourself out of the Eel," she said as Ann Marie folded herself stiffly into the chair opposite.

Rae slid a wine glass across and picked up the bottle of Cabernet. Ann Marie paled and shook her head. "I'm still getting over the other night."

Rae set the bottle down without comment.

"They'll be here in a few minutes," she said. "What's up?"

Ann Marie looked at her bleakly. Rae saw that she'd been crying. "What?" she said softly. "Honey. What happened?"

"Chris is seeing someone else," she said, her low voice almost inaudible.

"What?" Rae blurted, unbelieving. "No way! Are you sure?"

Ann Marie nodded, her face skull-like. "I'm sure. I found his diary. I wasn't looking for it," she rushed to add, as if Rae was about to accuse her of snooping. "I was tidying up the desk and there it was, 'lunch with Stephanie,' and I asked him about it and he told me. Everything."

Rae put her hand over Ann Marie's icy one. "What's 'everything'?" she asked. "Like…just lunch? Lunch is OK, isn't it?"

Ann Marie shook her head tightly. "Not just lunch. She…" She trailed off and looked down at their hands on the table in front of her. "She kissed him. That's how he put it, *she* kissed *him*. "

Rae hunched forward. "That's as far as it's gone? She kissed him?"

"That's enough, isn't it?" Ann Marie blurted. "Kissing someone else when you're, you're…" Her bottom lip contorted into a shapeless tremble and around it she forced "…married?"

Rae was silent as she looked into Ann Marie's ravaged face. "Of course,," she said softly. "But it wasn't like he slept with her. Is it?"

"He wanted to!"

"Did he say that?"

"He didn't have to. I could tell." Ann Marie was staring at her miserably. "What should I do?" she whispered. "I don't know what to do."

Rae rubbed her face with her free hand, struggling to understand her own reaction. Ann Marie had never confided in her about her marriage before. The few off-hand remarks Rae had made about men in her own life had never evoked from Ann Marie anything other than a ghostly smile and a change of subject. After a while Rae had gotten the message—that as a single woman she must hate men. And Ann Marie wasn't going to bash her man with a man-hater. That had hurt.

"Ann Marie, I can't tell you what to do in your marriage," she said finally. "All I can say is, you need to take care of yourself. You look like you haven't eaten or slept in days." Ann Marie lowered her eyes. Rae said, "Yeah, I thought so. Do you want to talk to someone, someone good? I can give you a number." Rae paused, expecting Ann Marie to recoil, but Ann Marie kept her head down and stared at the table.

Rae squeezed the hand she was still holding. "I'll call you with the number. And you call me any time."

The door blew open then and Cherrie burst in, Marla close behind her. Cherrie was giggling. Marla was scowling.

With a final squeeze Rae let go of Ann Marie's hand and moved over to let Cherrie sit down next to her. "Hi everyone," Cherrie said, and grabbed an empty wineglass and the Cabernet bottle. Marla pushed past an unresponsive Ann Marie to wedge herself into the chair against the wall. "Ditto hello," she said, and then, pointedly, to the side of Ann Marie's face, "Thanks for nothing."

Rae sighed and poured Marla a glass of wine.

"So," Cherrie said, a wine mustache staining her top lip. "Why are we here and not rehearsing tonight? "

Rae looked at each one of them in turn; Ann Marie wretched and immobile, Marla bristling, Cherrie blithe and self-absorbed. She took a deep breath. "I can't do this anymore," she said. "Particularly after Saturday. I...have to stop."

A stunned silence dropped over the table.

Into the shock Rae continued. "I work at this too much for too little return. I'm a nervous wreck. My day gig is suffering, I'm missing deadlines—" well, not really, but she had to stay up all night to make them "—and it's just not fun anymore."

"Well, if Cherrie would just not be such a slut—"

"Shut up, Marla!"

"Well, it's true. If you didn't give us all so much work to do trying to make you look good when you're late or drunk—"

"I do not!" Cherrie said, tears threatening.

"How's Mark by the way?" Ann Marie asked, rousing herself. "Remember him? Your husband?" This was something new. Ann Marie usually sided with Cherrie.

Cherrie stared at her, stung.

"Your problem," Marla said, "is you really do believe you're a diva."

"Yeah? Well, it wasn't me who blew it on Saturday!"

There was another uncomfortable silence. They all avoided looking at Ann Marie.

"You know what," Marla said. "I'm with Rae. I'm done with this. I work my ass off for this group and what do I get? Bupkis. It's Cherrie who gets all the attention, Cherrie everyone's worried about, Cherrie, Cherrie, Cherrie." She picked up her glass and drank it down. "I'm outta here."

"Good riddance!" Cherrie said.

Flushing, Marla reached her hand back in what looked like the wind-up to a slap. Rae snapped, "Enough!" She swept her gaze around the table. "Look at yourselves. You're acting like third graders! This has to stop!"

As one, they looked down.

Cherrie was the first to speak. "Are you really going to quit us?" she asked, the tears having overflowed and streaked her mascara. "Are you, Rae?"

Rae sighed and clutched at her hair. "As I said, this is just too much work. Do you know how long it took me to get that gig on Saturday?" They stared at her, an identical look of guilt stamped on each face. "Months. And now, big surprise, no one's returning my calls."

"So what!" Cherrie said, pursing her lips into her familiar pout. "We don't need any ol' artist collective or farmer's market to sing. We can just show up and do street corners, like we used to."

"Yeah, right," Marla said, but without heat. "And get roughed up by pit bulls. Or have you forgotten that fun little episode?"

Cherrie opened her mouth and then closed it.

Rae took a breath. "No, I wouldn't cancel on Ellen. Or you guys. No, I thought we could do that one gig and then we'd be done."

After that there didn't seem to be anything more to say. Marla left first, followed soon after by a sniffling Cherrie. As Ann Marie stood and gathered her things Rae said, "How're you feeling?"

"Better." Ann Marie managed a faint smile. "Thanks for listening to me." Then she, too, left.

Rae sat for a while and looked at her reflection in the darkened window next to her. Someone had shot a BB through it, fracturing it into a web of widening splinters, at its center a perfect hole. Rae gazed at the broken pieces of herself as raindrops splattered against and then rivuleted down the glass, some making it through the hole to pool inside on the sill.

But we did not come to Earth empty-handed. With an enormous crash that sounded throughout the universe the great glass was shattered into billions and billions of pieces. And each one of us, brought forth bleeding and crying into the enfolding arms of Earth, carried a shard of this glass with us, to look upon and see therein reflected our real selves, whole and exquisite and joyful and eternal.

The dining room of the North Coast Community Ecumenical Meeting Hall was a warm and aromatic refuge from the steady rain outside, filled with fleece-bundled, winter-booted, chatty people—as many kids as adults, it seemed. Rae pulled the door closed and brushed the rain off herself, trying to stay out of the way of Marla's umbrella on one side and Cherrie, vigorously shaking out her raincoat, on the other.

As she smoothed down her dress Marla leaned over. "God, I hate churches," she said. "I went to a Catholic girls' school for years. Nuns!" She shuddered.

"This isn't a real church," Rae said. "Well, not like that at least. They don't even have a pastor."

"Yeah, you said." Marla's mouth quirked. "But still."

Rae patted her shoulder, smiled at her, and looked around herself.

People were bustling back and forth getting the room ready for the holiday feast after the service. Roaming among them at knee height were several dogs in colorful hand-knit sweaters. Rae watched as one of them, wagging and gray-muzzled, camel-walk stiffly from person to person, mouth stretched into a dog smile, a knitted slipper sock tied jauntily to each paw. On the walls were hung posters celebrating Hanukah, Kwanzaa and Ramadan next to depictions of Jesus Christ and Santa Claus.

Rae hugged herself, shivering in her thin silk dress. The cold was concentrated mainly in her damp feet: she'd worn her strappy heels—cute but freezing. She wished she'd thought to wear rain boots and change here.

Suddenly from the busy crowd someone shouted, "The Divas are here!" the room cheered, and Rae was glad she was wearing her cold shoes. She glanced around at her little group. They looked surprised and pleased by the greeting. Even Ann Marie, her face wan and too thin, was smiling. Their last gig. Rae was glad it was for this cheerful gathering.

Ellen came over and handed them all mugs of something warm.

"Here," she said in her uniquely-accented English. "Put some meat on your bones."

Rae peered into her cup. "Huh?"

Ellen laughed her infectious laugh and, getting it, Rae joined in. Ellen was inviting her to get warm, not gain weight. "Thanks," Rae said, and drank deeply from the mug, which held spiced apple cider. The warmth seemed to go directly to her frozen toes. "Ah," she sighed. "Oh yes."

Ellen smiled at her, dimples flashing in her round cheeks and her black eyes shining with good humor. She was dressed in her usual many-colored skirts and wrap sweater, extra bells, beads and ribbons woven into her dreads in honor of the festivities. Against the day's colorless backdrop she was as vivid as a multi-ethnic mural. Impulsively Rae bent and enfolded her in a hug.

"Thank you for asking us to do this," Rae said huskily. "We're so glad to be here."

"Not a worry to you," Ellen said. "We are the ones excited." She chuckled comfortably and patted Rae's arm. "Not a worry."

"Rae! Rae!" Cherrie was behind her, whispering urgently. Rae turned and bent her head to hear her over the room's buzz. "Do you think they have any, you know, vodka or whiskey or something? To put into this?" She held up her mug and looked at Rae with undisguised need.

Cherrie's hair wasn't quite as mussed as it usually was on weekend morning gigs, and Rae had made her take off her sunglasses before they'd walked in, but her distress was obvious.

Rae shook her head wordlessly.

The last gig.

Over the room's noise a bell rang, and Ellen called out, "Now please come." It was time for the service.

"Oh God, here we go," Marla muttered. The room emptied out as people began moving down the passageway into the main hall. Rae took Ann Marie's arm, smiling at her, and they walked in with the rest of the congregation, dogs included.

The hall was washed with grey light streaming through the large windows that rimmed the upper half of the walls. The hall itself was a simple wooden structure with a high ceiling and exposed beams. The rustling of people settling themselves whispered inarticulately for a few moments and then quieted. Beautiful acoustics, Rae thought, perfect for unaccompanied voices.

They'd rehearsed the one carol they were to sing for the service until they knew the intricate harmonies of it by heart. A single carol sung to an attentive crowd, without distractions, in natural morning light, unaccompanied, un-amplified. No crutches. For a confident, well-rehearsed group of singers this situation would be a gratifying challenge. For the accident-prone it was fraught with limitless opportunities for calamity. Rae felt a familiar tightness gather in the center of her chest.

Not a worry to you, Ellen had said. Rae breathed slowly in and out.

The service began. Prayers were said, a group hymn sung, some community business about road closures was conducted. Cherrie began to rummage noisily in her purse, muttering to herself. Marla gave an audible sigh, looked at Rae and mouthed, "God." Ann Marie sat unmoving, staring straight ahead. Rae smiled at them. The last gig.

"And now," the main speaker said at last in his melodious voice, "it's time for the special musical number, a fifteenth century French carol, sung for us by the Divas."

Rae looked at the others, raised her eyebrows, and then stood and led the way down the center aisle of the hall and up onto the riser in the front. They arranged themselves into a half circle; as each singer got settled she gave a small nod. Rae raised the pitch pipe to her lips, blew the first note, and they all took a breath.

"O come O come thy Dayspring bright..."

Rae closed her eyes and opened her ears to Ann Marie's solid tenor, big and warm, and tuned to her, hearing only her for a few beats as the song grew, strengthened, and gathered her in.

"Pour on our souls thy healing light..."

Her eyes still closed, Rae heard Marla's clear harmony call to her, and she called back. They sang, entwined around each other, the notes coming impossibly close and then moving away, but always, always, together.

"Dispel the long night's ling'ring gloom..."

Then Cherrie's voice rose over them, sweet and rich and soaring, seeking them; and the weaving they'd made opened up, reached out—and they were one voice.

"And pierce the shadows of the tomb..."

Filled with the song now, wanting to include the listeners, Rae opened her eyes and was stunned by a sudden blinding brilliance. It filled the hall with blazing streaks that seemed to drop anchor in each person there, an infinitely-pointed star come to earth and hanging just outside the window above the hall's main entryway. Dazzled, she stared, and would have stopped singing, but the song reached out and drew her back in.

"Rejoice!"

Gazing out the window, light flooding her eyes but unable to look away, Rae sang, her voice coming from her without effort, strong and unrecognizable.

"Rejoice!"

The people seemed unaware of the light that filled the space around them and made long shadows along the hall's wooden floor. Backlit by a searing radiance they sat quiet and unmoving.

"Rejoice!"

The song was calling to her and, reluctantly, Rae closed her eyes again. It was ending now, the music quieting, their voices slowing to touch down together on one closing note; and then, at last, a final shared silence.

Rae opened her eyes. The room was back the way it had been. The people were sitting the way they'd been sitting all along. Rae looked down to find the stairs and realized her cheeks were covered with tears. As she led the way back up the aisle she swiped once at her face, stumbling into the pew, disoriented.

For the glass was in fact a mirror, and our time on earth was meant to fit the pieces of the mirror together to become, again, one with each other.

Marla came sidling into the pew after Rae and slouched down next to her, folding her arms. "Man, am I glad *that's* over with," she muttered. "God, I hate churches."

Still clutched by residual wonder, Rae stared at her, and then twisted herself around to look up through the window above the hall's entryway. The rain had stopped, a scrap of blue showing now through a tear in the clouds. She searched the rectangle of sky, bending around in her seat, and after a moment she saw distant movement. There, against the grey of the clouds, getting smaller and smaller as it rose, was a silver mylar balloon.

Author's Note

It's a mystery to me how some of the most warped, craven, cruel or otherwise horribly flawed human beings have managed to bring into existence some of the world's most sublime, soulful, healing and heart-stoppingly beautiful creations. This story is my attempt at a reckoning.

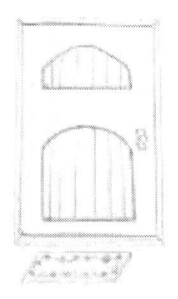

MISCAST

by Rick Markgraf

"Awright you mens, let's get nekkid!" Tom Carter grabbed the overhead molding and swung down the last few stairs into the men's dressing room. A chorus of friendly greetings came from within and he almost staggered from the heat and stale sweat odor that filled the long narrow space. "Damn, you guys smell bad. I mean really bad."

"Yeah and this is only the fourth week. Wait till week eight," said Frank Costello. Frank was closest to him and stood in a sleeveless undershirt and long white boxers. His legs were thin and looked unequal to the task of supporting his barrel-shaped body. His face was red and the color extended over the top of his head, only lightly obscured by the combed rows of pale gray hair. "This heat isn't helping any, either."

"Hey, Frankie, don't look now, but there's a tenor behind you," Tom said.

"Oh, jeez. I didn't see him," Frank joked. "Thanks, Tom, that was a close one."

Bill Waters' long yellow locks poked through the linen shirt he was pulling on, until they could see him grinning back at them. "If you stout fellows could sing more than three notes in any key, they might make you a tenor, too."

"No, thanks. I've heard how they make tenors. None of that for me." Tom walked to the long closet pole that stretched the length of the room. He found the wooden hanger with his costume on it and started undressing. Several others came in and the room grew closer, with men standing side by side, bumping each other with elbows and butts as they pulled on or off the various articles of clothing. "Hey," Tom said, to no one in particular. "Didn't we have a fan in here? What happened to the fan?"

"Yeah," someone replied from the other side of the hanging costumes, "The women's fan died and Corky took ours upstairs to them. Something about the wigs wilting."

"Well, damn! I don't want to sound unchivalrous, God forbid, but somebody could die down here. Frankie's close to a heart attack already anyway. I'm thinking maybe I should go up there and get it back."

"Yeah, sure. That's a great way to get a heart attack. You might see some of those old birds in their skivvies." Marvin Atkins was bent over next to Tom pulling a pair of tights over his legs. The tights were obviously several sizes too small for the huge calves Marvin was trying to stuff into them.

"Yes, there's danger in that, it's true." Tom affected a medieval accent. "Yet, perchance fair maiden will grace my presence in less formidable attire. Besides, anything is better than your ugly bu …"

"Everybody out for practice!" Corky, the stage manager, yelled at the stairs adjoining the dressing rooms. As a group, in various stages of dress, the men filed up the stairs, through the Green Room, and out onto the stage of the ancient auditorium. The lights were up in the theater, and they could see the rows of connected metal seats stretching off to the back wall. Covered in thickly padded vinyl of dark red, the seats were soft enough, but far too narrow for most adults to rest comfortably for long.

"Ah! Air! I had forgotten it could be so thin," Tom quipped.

The women filed in behind, laughing and chatting until Sally, the musical director, spoke up. "Ok, let's start loosening up. Do mi sol mi do," she sang, and the piano played two chords, with the second chord half an octave higher. She pitched her voice to match as the entire group joined in with her. "Do mi sol mi do!" Chord, Chord. Up the scale she went until most of the group dropped out, unable to reach the note. Then she began working down the scale into the regions where only the deepest bass voice could sing.

"Okay, just a few comments. Chorus, remember to round your tones when you sing 'Wooing, happy be'. Some of you were really nasal on the 'be' during rehearsal. Sing it, don't tweet it." She ignored the series of tweets from the men's chorus, and the responding giggles from teens in the women's chorus. "And I hope you've all been practicing the words. I saw some of the men still singing 'Watermelon' last week. It's nice to keep your mouths moving, but this is the fourth week, for Pete's sake. You may be amateurs, but please don't act like amateurs."

She excused the chorus, but held some of the lead singers for further comments. Tom trooped down the stairs with the rest of the men and finished donning his costume, a linen shirt with brilliant sash, baggy pants made of some paisley drapery material, a brown vest and bandanna, with black eye patch. "Hey, who took my hat? I left it right here," he said.

"Is this it? I found it on the floor and didn't know where it came from," Bill replied.

"Yeah, don't you try to steal my hat. That's not a tenor hat. That's a real swashbuckling pirate's hat. A manly hat. It's a manly, manly thing we do. A manly thing."

"Yeah, well, you'd better watch out for your manly thing or I'll cut it off with my rapier."

"Oh yeah? My rapier's bigger than your rapier."

"Benson!" Corky yelled from the foot of the stairs. "Is Benson here? Anybody seen Benson? He didn't check in."

"He's not in here."

"Haven't seen him."

"Nope."

"Shit fire. He's on in the first act. If he comes in let me know." Corky left quickly, shaking his head and waving a clipboard.

"Jawohl, mein Fuhrer," mumbled Frankie.

"Stage Nazi is in a snit again. Looks like he lost a star," said Bill.

"Yeah, well, he might have a problem, but who are we going to sing to if Benson's not there. I'm thinking we might have a problem, too." Tom grabbed a bottle of Fabreze and sprayed the armpits of his costume. "Floyd's his neighbor, isn't he? Hey Floyd, did you see Benson before you left Fortuna?"

Floyd Carter walked up from behind a row of half-dressed men. His grey goatee and tall lean figure made him look almost regal. In a deep bass voice he replied, "I think he went fishing this morning. I saw him loading a plastic bucket and a surf rod into his pickup truck. Just waved at me, and I didn't ask him where he was going."

Corky yelled down the stairs again. "House is open. Let's keep it quiet now. Anybody seen Benson yet?"

"No," all the men yelled in unison.

"Holy horseshit," Corky groaned. "What are we going to do for a Pirate King? Where's the Director? Is Chris down there?"

"No," all the men yelled in unison.

"Hey, keep it quiet, will you?"

"No," all the men yelled in unison.

Corky left, shaking his head and waving a clipboard.

Gerry Benson awoke, disoriented, wet to the bone, and shivering so hard his teeth clacked together painfully. His nose and scalp were filled with wet gritty sand and tasted, or smelled, he couldn't recognize which, of fish, crab or seaweed. An impulse grew within his gut and he vomited acrid seawater into the sand. He lay there, gasping for oxygen from tortured lungs, until the cold swish of a wave intruded on his feet, legs, and torso. In terror, his body convulsed its way further up the sand, every muscle pulsing at capacity to assist. Exhausted, he lost his tenuous grip on consciousness and lapsed into fretful dreams of momentous trials.

"So, Frankie, is your father here tonight?" Tom said.

"Huh, I guess so. He hasn't missed a performance since we started. I don't think he's ever missed a show since this place opened."

"So, how's his Gilbert & Sullivan?"

"You kidding? He knows them all by heart. Sings them in the garden, in the shower. Even at the bowling alley. It's a little embarrassing."

"Why don't you ask him to come back here and try on Benson's uniform, just in case?"

"Ok, but Benson had better not show up, or Papa Costello will sap him from behind and leave him in the wings."

"Yeah, well, Benson's a trouper. If he could be here, he'd be here now. I'm kinda worried about him." Tom used the end of his scarlet sash to mop sweat from his forehead and neck. "I'm going to go tell Chris we found a sub."

Tom took the stairs three at a time and found Chris on the far side of the curtained stage, arguing in a whisper with his stage manager, Corky. Chris's left hand was waving wildly, while his right arm, held horizontal by a plaster cast, bounced around in an effort to keep up.

"Hey Chris," Tom said in a quiet voice. "Problem solved, I think. If Benson doesn't show, we can sub in Frank's daddy. He knows all the Gilbert and Sullivan plays, and has a pretty good baritone. He's in the audience again."

"Papa Costello?" Chris said, "Are you kidding me? He's gotta be 80."

"Naw, he's only 75. I went to his birthday party. And who else can do the part?

"I could do it. I did it before."

"Not with a cast on. You'd knock your leading lady out of the ring, and then where would we be? We need Costello or we won't have a show. You want to refund all those tickets?"

Chris was silent, and Corky waved his clipboard in the air, shook his head, and said, "Better get him in costume, he's on in 15 minutes".

"Damn Benson," Chris said as he turned to stride across the stage. Tom ducked as Chris' right sailed past his head.

"Yeah, you're welcome," Tom whispered at his director, knowing he wasn't heard.

Tom started back toward the dressing room as the five-piece orchestra began to tune up in the pit. He stopped at the wings, pulled back the curtain a little and looked out at the audience. "Wow, good crowd tonight," he thought. "Hope we can pull this off." He noticed the vacant seat in the front row, and assumed it had held Papa Costello. His heart fell as he recognized the man in the next seat. Vincent Edmunds, the local art critic, small, aquiline and silver-haired, sat primly in the front row. His column in the Times-Standard could make or break their chances of future attendance.

Papa Costello was in his thin white undershirt and long john bottoms. Frank was tugging the long-sleeved linen shirt over his head. "Sorry about the stench down here, Papa," Tom said. "They keep a herd of billy goats in here when we aren't using it."

"I haven't been able to smell anything in ten years," said Papa. "A little goat smell would be welcome."

"Actually," said Frank, "Billy goats smell a lot better than this. Tom was understating it."

"So Papa, do you know any lines in Pirates? Because we have an art critic in the audience tonight."

"Hell yes. I know all the G. and S. shows. Used to play with LOTS when I was younger. That's all they did. They were a quality bunch, they were."

"Ah, I don't know who that is," said Tom.

"That's because you are a rookie. You don't know nothing. The Light Opera Theater of Sacramento, LOTS, was the best damn opera group in California. Least, they were when I was there."

"I played two shows with LOTS when I was going to school there," said Bill. With makeup kit in hand he was doing his best to darken Papa's eyebrows. "Papa's right. They are a quality group. My ecology professor and his wife ran the show and played in it too."

"Interlude." Corky's whisper was nearly as loud as if he had yelled. "All first leads on stage, chorus in the green room. Papa, do you need me to cue you on the words?"

"How about I cue you?" Papa said as he took the stairs two at a time. "Your mama was sucking her thumb when I first played this part."

"Uh-huh, that was a long time ago. When was the last time you played it?"

"Oh, she was probably into bigger things by then." Papa turned his back on Corky and took his place on the stage. He suddenly seemed larger, bolder, younger.

The orchestra finished the interlude and the heavy curtain began to rise. Corky shook his head and hung his clipboard on a hook. He settled in the wings on a tall wooden stool and studied the stage book lying open on its shelf under a miniscule blue light.

In the Green Room, chorus members and leads were scattered about in ancient folding chairs, standing or sitting on the pale vinyl floor with their backs against the wall. Bill Waters stood facing a dark window, mouthing the words to a song while keeping time with his right hand. Floyd Carter was slumped in a chair with his eyes closed, his lips moving rapidly, emitting a low grumble of unintelligible lyrics. Most of the women's chorus were seated on chairs, except for one teen who sat on the floor reclining against the shoulder of her current stage romance. The frothy white dresses of the women contrasted with the colorful costumes of the pirates scattered among them.

The Rain All Day Writers

"What do you figure happened to Benson?" Frankie asked as he retrieved a diet cola from the jaws of a vending machine.

"I hope he didn't get sucker-punched by a rogue wave," said Tom. "That sort of thing can ruin your day."

"Yeah, I know. I climbed up over the South Jetty on the bay side and arrived just in time for a set of two big ones. I was lucky enough to have a rock to duck behind. My wife took a picture just as a wave shot up over my head about ten feet high. I was soaked through. Put out my cigar, too. She thought it was funny, but she didn't feel how hard it hit the rock in front of me. Could have knocked me onto the rocks behind like I would flick a fly." Frankie cocked his finger and flicked it toward Tom's nose. "That ocean can be scary even when you know what you're doing."

"Not much we can do, I guess. I wouldn't even know where to look, even if I wasn't doing a show." Tom looked down at his feet thoughtfully.

"Tough call." Frankie said. "We don't have enough to go on. If we knew where Benson was, it would be worth taking a look to see if his pickup was there. But with what we have now I can't see leaving the show in the lurch to go hunt for him."

"I agree, but it really bugs me that I don't know what's happened to him. Could just be a flat tire, but it also could be some serious karma coming down on him. I wish I knew what to do."

Corky appeared suddenly, interrupting their thoughts. In a loud whisper he told them it was time to come to the wings for the chorus' entrance. Tom and Frankie followed Bill behind the rear curtain to the far wings, creeping sideways slowly to avoid disturbing the backcloth with their passage. As one, the actors paused to think about their places and actions on the stage, and then, when the music reached the proper place, strode onto the stage singing their pirate's song.

It was their place to portray themselves as drunken pirates, and they enjoyed the part to its fullest. Slurring their lyrics and swinging their flagons, they wove around the stage to their assigned places. They became a scurrilous, drunken, lecherous lot of the worst blackguards, emphasized by their actions and expressions, abetted by the lyrics and music. A transformation occurred. Their voices joined in multiple parts and tones and became one. Each of them felt it, created it, as their own tones combined with the multiple, blended and augmented, bass with baritone and alto, threaded with the sweet high notes of the tenor and soprano until all were in crescendo. The response of the audience was mountainous, and fed them with its thunder of appreciation.

"Damn, that was sweet," said Tom as he entered the Green Room. "That, for the critic, let him moan for his own untasted dreams."

"It's why we are here," Bill said. " I don't get that at my day job."

"You've got a day job? Tom jabbed at Bill's upper arm. "Who in God's name would hire a tenor? You never did tell me what you do for a living."

"Yeah, well, it's not something I talk about a lot. It's just a living."

"C'mon. Spring. Nobody up here is proud of what they work at to keep their aspirations alive. I'm a waiter, for cripes sake. It's not what I will be doing when I'm sixty."

"Well, since you ask. I'm a bouncer at the casino. Security guard during the day shifts, but they've been putting me on late recently. After the show I get to go on the hill and card the teenies and bounce the drunks."

"What? But you're a tenor. Where is their sense of propriety? Tenors don't bounce, they prance. How can you be a tenor who bounces?"

"Tae Kwan Do, Grasshopper," said Bill. "I've been a black belt for five years. I don't really bounce, but I do persuade. It doesn't usually require good vocal capabilities."

"That's what I hate about shows," Tom said, "You never really know who you are insulting. Sometimes I long for the good old days when all the tenors were nerds or ninety-seven pound weaklings. The world is going to Hell in a hand basket. It's like you can't trust anybody anymore."

"I grok that," said Bill. "My roommate dumped me for a bodybuilder last week. I'll probably never be the same. What are you doing after the show?"

"What?" said Tom. "I'm not that kind of guy."

"Me neither. Gotcha."

"Chorus in the wings," Corky whispered at the top of his lungs. "Act two."

Gerry Benson awoke to a cold such as he had never known. His body temperature had fallen drastically, aided by inaction, exhaustion, and the 40 degree water of the northern Pacific Ocean. Immersed in the water, he would not have survived more than a half hour before succumbing to hypothermia. The cold fog-laden air on Centerville Beach was warm by comparison, but he was dangerously close to unconsciousness, and without assistance death would inevitably follow.

In a moment of lucidity, he rolled onto his back, and felt the uncomfortable bulge of his cell phone beneath him, pouched at the hip in its belt case. His bones ached with the cold, but some primeval urge exerted against a modern reflex caused him to reach for the phone, a ruggedized waterproof model named the Boulder. Gerry pushed buttons, unaware and uncaring which were activated. He put it to his ear and listened as it rang four times, and then there was a message he could not make out against the rush of surf. He barely found strength to mumble. "Centerville. Way up. Help." The speaker eventually responded with another message, followed by a beeping tone. Gerry did not hear.

"Hey, what about the cast party? Did anyone call Big Louie's?" Frankie was sweating from the exertion of changing and the intricate dance he had performed as a Keystone Cop in the last scene before the intermission.

Tom had not had a part in that scene, and replied, "I'll do it." He descended the stairs into the heavy air of the dressing room and retrieved his cell phone from his trousers. Immediately, he saw he had a voice message from Gerry Benson. "Ah! About time you made your excuses," he thought. A chill descended over him as he heard the sea-soaked voice of Gerry Benson, partially disguised by the pounding of surf.

Bounding up the stairs, he found Tony Costello and blurted his message. "Benson needs help on Centerville, way up. I'm going to go. You bring everybody after the show. I'll light a fire so you can find us."

As he raced to the parking lot, Tom pushed the send button on his cell phone, dialing Gerry's number from the display. He listened as it rang, one, two, three, and then an answer. It was a croak, really, but it was Benson's croak and relief flooded through him. The voice at the other end was shaky. "Who's this? I can't see without my glasses."

"Gerry, it's Tom Carter. I just got your message. Are you OK?"

"Wet. Cold. But I'm getting warmer, I think. Glad I dressed warm. I got hit by a wave. Not sure where I am. Somewhere up Centerville Beach. I lost my glasses and I can't see anything."

"Do you want the Coasties, Gerry? I can have a chopper there in ten minutes. I'll be there in twenty. "

"I don't think so. Twenty minutes ago I might have said yes, but I'm going to be OK and that would cost a bundle. I just want a fire."

"You got it buddy. Sing a sea shanty. I'll be there before you know it."

"Enough of the sea for a while. Push it, will you?"

"You got it, pal. I'll call when I hit the beach."

Tom had the Super Beetle up to ninety on the freeway and took the back roads past Ferndale at top speed. He had to slow for the curves near Centerville, and prayed the deer would stay off the road. The pale green glow of Gerry Benson's recycled Park Service pickup appeared in his headlights as he neared the beach parking lot. He barely slowed when he hit the sand and the light beetle churned up on top. He was grateful for the heavy fog that had kept the sand damp and supportive. This was no time to get stuck. As he reached the band of wet sand above the breakers, he saw the tide was receding. That was a stroke of luck. The beach at Centerville had steep banks that would challenge the traction of the wheels, but he was able to choose his path and stay on the wet sand.

Tom knew better than to give in to impatience. The headlights rose and fell with his motion over the peaks and valleys of the sand, and in rushing, he might accidentally miss seeing Gerry … might even run over him. He called again and was grateful when he heard Gerry's answer. "I see your lights,"

Gerry said. His voice sounded hoarse, so Tom knew he had swallowed and inhaled salt water. "I can't tell how far away, because of the fog, and I probably couldn't anyway without my glasses. I can hear your engine now, so it's probably another quarter mile. Look for a log, about twenty feet long with a root star at the end. Damn, it's cold."

"Almost there, buddy. Help is on the way." Tom saw the log, first, and then he saw Gerry sitting on the sand, arms wrapped around his knees in an attempt to hold in the heat. He stopped and popped the release on the boot. In a moment, he was at Gerry's side with a blanket.

"We'd better get you into the veedub, Gerry. The heater fan is broken, so it won't be much help, but I'll have a fire going real soon and it will warm you up. Meanwhile, suck on this." Tom produced a stainless steel flask from the boot and unscrewed the top for him. "It won't make you warmer, but it will help your throat feel better."

"Oh, God bless you, Tom. Nectar of the Gods"

With Gerry in the front passenger seat, Tom retrieved a magnesium safety flare from the boot. In the light from the headlights, he ranged up onto the dunes and grabbed an armful of small driftwood sticks. He tossed them against the log and struck the match end of the flare, thrusting it into the pile, before casting about for larger pieces of driftwood. By the time he returned, the sticks had caught and flared enough to light the rest. In five minutes, the fire was large enough that Gerry opened the door and moved to it, stomping his feet, and collapsing onto the log beside the fire. Tom killed the headlights and then left a message on Frankie's cell to reassure him. He rejoined Gerry at the fire, which was now a robust bonfire.

"So, why did you decide to take a swim in this weather and at this time of night?"

"Do you want any of this stuff?" Gerry said. "It's almost gone."

"Naw, you need it more than I do. You can buy me a drink later."

"Gladly, but it could never taste half as good as this. It wasn't night. It was late afternoon, and I was on my way back to my truck with a bucket full of two-pounders. I'd been watching the waves, of course. I fished this beach most of my life without a problem. I was crossing a low spot, where the waves angle up to the center and cross each other. Suddenly I got hit from one crossing behind me. Never heard a thing, just Bam! and I was moving fast in deep water. I was sure I was dead. Couldn't swim with all the heavy clothing. Couldn't stand up cause the water was too deep and fast. I think I did drown. Passed out underwater. Next thing I know I'm waking up on the beach with my nose and mouth and everything else full of wet sand and seawater. I've thrown a lot of fish back, but this is the first time they've returned the favor."

Talking seemed to make his throat worse, because Gerry tipped the flask up on end and swallowed the last of the whisky. "Ahh, that burns so good. You look like a pirate."

"Oh, yeah. I didn't take time to change out of my costume. Figured you wouldn't want to wait for me."

"Well, it fits in real well. You couldn't have chosen better props, especially if you imagine the veedub is a boulder. I guess I missed the show, huh?"

"No, you were there. Papa Castillo subbed in for you. He was doing pretty well, too. Good thing because Vince Edmunds was sitting in the front row."

"Edmunds, huh? We are luckier than you think, then. Edmunds hates me and pans every show I'm in. Seems he thought the woman I married was his girlfriend. They dated in high school. Hard to believe when you look at him now. I guess he didn't age well."

"Well, timing is everything. I guess we should thank you for trying to drown yourself. How are you feeling now? I see you are steaming nicely. We'll have to turn you soon so you don't get overdone."

"In a few. I'm feeling better but I want to cook through two thirds of the way before I turn and get the last third."

"Are you hungry? I have a bag of Costco jerky in the boot. I keep it for emergencies, and this might well qualify as such."

"Bring it on, please. A portion of filet mignon could not be welcomer. I'm afraid I lost my lunch along with copious amounts of sea water."

With their mouths filled with the tough peppery meat, neither of them spoke for awhile. Gerry finally turned his back to the fire. Tom retrieved some more firewood from the dunes. They rested for a while, silently gazing at the flames.

"I believe I see some headlights on the beach," Tom said at last. "We may be enjoying some company before long."

Through the fog, multiple headlights bobbed like fireflies trapped in cheesecloth. Soon, the throb of engines filled the air and they could make out the outlines of several quad runners highlighted by four-wheel drive vehicles driving behind. The vehicles lined up around the fire and disgorged a large crew of men clad in pirate garb.

"Looks like the Coliseum parking lot after a Raiders game," said Gerry.

"Aargh, that's a right fine fire, mateys." Frankie Costello slogged through the sand, bandana wrapped around his head, with a prop knife clenched between his teeth. Soon, the fire was surrounded by a host of pirates and maidens in white.

Papa Costello, in the frock coat and cocked hat of a pirate king, dismounted from the back of a quad-runner and joined them. He slapped Gerry on the back and said, "Chasing mermaids, were you, Benson? I hope you caught an extra one for me. I've been working hard while you were out for a swim with the fishies." The sound of a motor made them all look up as a straggler appeared through the fog. A Suzuki Samurai came into view, turned 180 degrees, and backed up toward the fire.

"Ah, I see Stage Nazi has arrived with the treasure," said Frankie. "We sent one of his crew over early to get the pizza and beer. Drownings are one thing, but you can't expect pirates to give up their cast party."

As he opened the back of the little SUV, Corky shook his head, and began singing in a reedy tenor, quickly joined by the thunderous voices of all.

"A rollicking band of pirates, we
Who, tired of tossing on the sea
Are trying our hand at a burglary
With weapons grim and gory!"

Author's Note

This story is born of the love I have for community theater. Working closely for months with a disparate group of volunteers develops camaraderie and they become a family of strangers. You come to love these strangers, like a family, for their peculiarities and talents, their creativity, their dedication, and yes, for their flaws. It is also a grand time sink.

The story offers respectful recognition of the dangers inherent in the ocean I love so much. In my study of this ocean, I have sailed on its surface, dove beneath it, and explored its beaches, jetties, and tide pools. I have been surprised and inundated by waves crashing from high over my head, saved only by the shield of a convenient rock. Anyone who feels firsthand the ocean's power is humbled by it forever.

AUTHOR BIOGRAPHIES

LISA BANEY

Lisa Baney first began making up stories when she was a small girl and the next door neighbor lady apparently believed her about the talking deer walking out of the forest and hanging around with her all day. Later, in the fifth grade, she wrote her first full-length story, a rather opaque science fiction piece entitled "But The Girl Was Gone," based very loosely on the Roy Thinnes character from the TV series "The Invaders." Later still she was bedeviled by writer's block, managing only to produce about a story and a half every ten years or so. Membership in the Rain All Day Writers has changed all that.

TONY WESTKAMPER

Tony Westkamper is the group's newest member. He has two sons who have graduated out of the house, a wife, Sally, two dogs, and the world's scruffiest one eyed cat.

Originally trained as a nuclear reactor operator in the US Navy, he has worked as an electronics technician for over 40 years. Other interests are digital nature photography, gardening, insects, metal work, and riding his motorcycle.

He lives in the country like a troll among the redwoods, fighting off hordes of giant yellow banana slugs. When he was very young an evil English-teacher-witch laid a curse on him. He has been writing ever since. He once wrote an article which was published in a trade journal on imaging the tooth of a mammoth with a CT scanner.

JUNE NESSLER

June Nessler is a charter member of the Rain All Day Writers. She came to Humboldt County from Philadelphia, Pennsylvania, in 1961. As a Registered Nurse, she worked at Trinity Hospital (now Mad River Hospital) in Arcata while attending Humboldt State College (now Humboldt State University) to finish her degree in music which began as a science degree at Temple University in Philadelphia. Eventually she obtained her teaching credential and taught junior high school at Fortuna Town School until her retirement in 1992. Meanwhile she raised son Robert and daughter Elisán who have made her very proud. She has participated in various local musical and theatrical productions. Music has given way to writing as the major pastime in her life. In 2010 she and her best friend, husband Bob, moved to Redding, California, to be near family.

SHARI SNOWDEN

Shari Snowden is a native Californian who grew up in the southern region before drifting north. She graduated from Chapman University and was a social worker and counselor for many years. She wrote opinion pieces for her local newspaper and grant proposals for social service programs before plunging into fiction, poetry, and lyrics. She and her husband, John, have two daughters and two granddaughters, and enjoy exploring beautiful and mysterious places, especially the North Coast.

RICK MARKGRAF

Rick Markgraf lives with his wife and high school sweetheart, Carol, in the small town of Fortuna, near the banks of the Eel River. Writing is a beloved hobby for him, and he has spent years developing his craft. The business of publishing holds less interest, and so this is the first time his works have been produced for public display. Rick retired after twenty-five years at the University of California, Davis, most recently as manager of the department of Environmental Science and Policy. In his varied careers he has been a microscope repair technician, a hospital supply clerk, roofer, service station attendant and Operations NCO at a school for National Guard armory technicians. He holds a Bachelor's degree in Marine Biology and has always loved the ocean, a primary motivation for moving to the North Coast. He currently works as Purchaser for the Humboldt County Office of Education.

CECELIA HOLLAND

Cecelia Holland grew up on the east coast but came to Humboldt County 35 years ago and has never left, raising her three daughters among the redwoods and the frogs and the rainbows. A lifelong writer, she has written more than 30 novels, mostly historical fiction. The Rain All Day Writers Group was her idea and she is very proud of it. She keeps chickens, cats and goats, spends time with her children and grandchildren, travels much, and wrestles every day with the English language, which she considers one of the greatest inventions of the human mind.

ALINE FABEN

Aline was born and grew up in Chicago, went to college in Minnesota, taught high school English in Hartford, Connecticut and Chicago, went to graduate school in Buffalo, New York. She lived in central Illinois, taught college in South Carolina, and then moved to San Diego, where she began a 25 year career selling college textbooks. Moving to beautiful Humboldt County in retirement in 2004, she plans never to move again! She lives in Fortuna with her partner, Eric Furman, a metal sculptor. Since retiring she has knitted more than ever before, and learned to spin yarn. Aline has enjoyed writing since fifth grade, when her teacher, Mrs. Reese, asked her to write a description of a scenic photograph. She wrote poetry during high school and college, but in the last few years has written short stories, a novel, and memoir.

MONICA HUBBARD

Monica Hubbard moved to Humboldt for the weather.

Made in the USA
Charleston, SC
12 July 2011